Ancient Steel:
Scry Tharg Rises

Ancient Steel: Scry Tharg Rises

A Novel by

David C. Kennedy

To order additional copies of this book, contact:
Xlibris LLC
1-888-795-4274
www.Xlibris.com
Orders@Xlibris.com
135597

This Book Is Dedicated To My Wife
Cynthia Trickett Froude Kennedy, the Encourager

CHAPTER ONE

THERE WAS DIRT and ash in the wound. His arm was starting to turn a sickly, dark green. The tall swordsman leaned with one boot on the base of his spaceship and pushed a thin, hollow needle through the vein. Nearly vertically above him three Scaderkian Moons were a soft, fuzzy, black. With his heart still pumping his chest in and out like a forge bellows, his blood was coming out of his arm in brief, and regular fan-shaped arcs. He was getting very dizzy, but, as usual, he tried to force himself not to throw up. Blood and worms always made him want to vomit. He held his breath as he twisted the acutorsion needle around in the ugly, deep gash, trying to find the right angle for stopping blood loss, as he had so many times before. His mouth opened in a grimace of pain, yet he did not cry out. He was silent except for an occasional involuntary sob. He wasn't sobbing because of the stomach-turning pain the dirty needle was creating in the lip-shaped wound, but because of his daughter Carla. He always thought of her after every battle, every duel, every war. He'd sob and mutter, "Oh Carol I miss you so my small one." He had long ago forgotten her real name had been Carla. That happens when you haven't seen a loved one for four thousand years.

"Pilate's fist!" he swore at the sudden explosion of sharp, raw torture in his festering arm. He thought of Belinda, his 1990 Harley Davidson, a 1340 Fat Boy touring motorcycle he kept in mint shape on board his ship. He had found that thinking of something beautiful when he suffered often helped ease the pain. This calmed him at once. Even though the fight had ended only seconds ago, the Scaderk warrior had used a merc-blade with stinger poison needles on all three edges. The poison, from the Yasha plant in the river of the same name on Caf, caused instant gangrene in an open wound. The pain from the powerful slash felt even worse as he finally stopped the bleeding and pulled out the needle. He wiped it off on his soft leather dueling jacket and pushed it back into the sponge brick in the small opening at the foot of his landing gear. He passed his bloody palm over the sponge and the blue metal plate sucked shut in the odd plop-like sound of the ship's water-based pneumatics.

The familiar sound woke the Scaderk soldier nearby who tried to extend the stump of his spinal arm to where his severed claw still held his deadly blade. But the transparent fluid pouring out of the ruined extremity was now so deep that the errant body part actually floated farther away on it. "I knew you weren't as fast as they said you were Tharg" he squeaked out, a metallic thought aimed in the tall human's direction. "If so, I couldn't have added that little nick to your legendary repertoire of wounds," this last utterance couched in contempt and derision, but also, awe. "You're dead. Die. Tharg whispered sadly. "Die." The Scaderk officer stretched his broken form into an arc over the muddy battleground trying to find some vestige of power left to move or act, but Tharg had cut him to pieces and he was nearly vapour. "I will die Scry Tharg" he squeaked, but perhaps I'll take you with me, Master Swordsman!" again with contempt, sarcasm. Tharg looked down at the broken fighter. He had been fast, faster than most. Lasted almost a full second. I must be getting old he thought. "I'll give you peace if you wish". He offered in his strange, sad whisper. So famous throughout the galaxies, the undergrounds of the worlds and even, back on Earth. Suddenly he bent down and flicked the clips of his long, brown leather boots and kicked them off. He then did the most alien thing the Scaderk had ever screened an Earthling doing. The haggard looking duellist reached into his landing pod. There was a pneumatic hiss and he pulled his arm out holding an old, beat up square of earth wood. He placed it gently on the mud before him and stepped on it in his bare feet. He looked at his only observer dying there in the mud nearby and said, "I'm not concerned about your Severn Flights Scaderk." He then lifted one leg after the other in a curious dancelike pattern while at the same time singing to himself, "Oh crawdaddy fish. Oh crawdaddy fish. "In his youth, the Scaderk had learned the folklore of Scry Tharg, the immortal swordfighter. He knew well the fable of his mysterious dance, performed after each victory, but he had always believed it was nothing more than folklore, silly human propaganda. He felt sudden emotion surge within, a sense of overwhelming loss, of power, of the ability to act. Oddly he couldn't fight the notion that it was fitting and proper for him to die this way, at the hands of Scry Tharg, the four thousand year old swordfighter, the Whistler, the Hunter, the Rider, the Christmas Boy, and all the other titles Tharg bore. Indeed, curiously, the Scaderk felt good about the way he would go. Even, honoured. His long life, seven Earth years, formidably long for the violent Scaderk was seeping inexorably into the periphery of time mist.

Suddenly he was overwhelmed by loneliness. It went away quickly when he remembered the Severn Flights, also legendary, but this time a true Scaderk phenomenon. The very real and indestructible ghosts of Scaderks past who attacked and always viciously destroyed any who dared kill a Victorial Scaderk soldier. As Captain of the Republican Tower Guard he could expect an astonishing force of Severn's to flay Tharg until he was nothing but Illipitian flinders. He almost squeaked out an Earthling laugh in Tharg's honour but was instantly disgusted by the thought and the dirty human habit. "Your abominable four thousand years are coming to a dark and horrific end Earth thing," he managed to clink out in failing, tinfoil thought. Then . . . yes! He could hear the horror coming. Coming for the man. The crazy human freakling. The thousands of beating wings that so many Scaderkian enemies had heard in the ticking instant just before they looked up in horror to see the famous wings of Hell fly into their screaming mouths. Blood, as always, took its payment and he clicked off forever with the sight of Tharg swinging his instrument of pain, his ugly blue blade up into the air at something all-powerful and soul-hungry coming down from the Scaderkian night-sky at his pitifully human countenance. Their speed was soundblur. The last thing the rather worthy Scaderk warrior heard caused him great sadness for some inexplicable reason. He heard Tharg say, even as his sword blurred with spacerub speed up toward the incoming Flights, "I pray it is so, Scaderk, I pray it is so."

A little while later as he lay in his flight tube waiting for it to fill with liquid oxygen he started to wonder, as he had many times before, how he had ever gotten so out of touch with reality. The irony of his existence couldn't make him grin however, as he thought of all those humans and indeed, other races, who spent so much time in research, study and prayer, trying to find some way to beat death and live forever. He was living forever and he hated it beyond redemption, as someone he couldn't remember used to say. His flight tube filled, he reached down by his naked thigh and pulled back the vellum-covered seal bar. He was sealed in a heated tube, breathing purified liquid-oxygen, his preferred method of vast distance travel. He would sleep in a few bits when the artificial intelligence of his Nova class space ship launched into a pre-set flight plan for the Maison Neuf galaxy, the mortal enemies of the Scaderk nation. There he would get his reward for the duel with the Vitorial Guard Captain. Getting a reward of unknown nature was the only thing in the universe and his existence that he found mildly interesting. It was always a part of his contract no matter if he was signing on for a war, or a duel or an assassination or even a proxy execution. The agency hiring him had to agree to reward him with something he would find interesting. In a Universe in which Tharg was famous and legend for his boredom this was a great challenge and risk for those who wanted to hire his skills and his immortality. Because if he didn't like his reward he had the legal right to identify the nation and its location to the Endurions, a species whose only reason for existence was to conquer the known and unknown worlds. Nobody ever knew what actually happened to those in the past who had failed to interest him with his reward. The seal-bar locked into position and Tharg immediately began to fall into scriff-induced sleep. It would take precisely ninety-three seconds. As the familiar out-of-body lightness began to take over his consciousness Tharg began again, to try to recall how he had ended up like this, how he had come to this blood-calloused life of his. It was so hard to remember . . . was there a big hall somewhere? Lights . . . singing . . . old friends . . . a beginning or . . . an ending . . .

Thirty seven year old Scott Robert Thorne crossed his long legs and sat back on the old chrome chair, put his elbows on the small round table before him and absorbed the night, the evening, the party, his life. It was New Year's Eve, 1999. All Hallow's School Hall in Corner Brook, Newfoundland (a huge rock in the North Atlantic off the East Coast of Canada) glowed in the soft warm dusk of a thousand candles. The combination of cigarette smoke and the vague yellow fuzz of the candles fell like clouds of sunshine falling on the room full of couples dancing, talking, remembering. A huge speaker system played a slow, mesmeric tune called Sensitive Kind by J-J. Cale. Although many couples danced the slow dance with arms around each other, each of them was in a trance of their own private kind, intimidated by the date and the night and what was coming in a few hours. The Year Two Thousand! Two thousand! Everybody was sad, reticent, lethargic, and it wasn't the booze.

It was the night, this night. The passing of an age in an instant, a few hours hence. Goodbye The Sixties. Goodbye the two World Wars. Goodbye Hitler. Goodbye Kennedy. Goodbye Jim Morrison, John Lennon, Elvis, Marilyn Monroe, O. J. Simpson – Goodbye Lincoln! Shakespeare for God's sake! Scott absorbed the night like an addict absorbs the onset of a hit. He kept closing and opening his eyes like a drunk who can't stay awake after one too many. He sipped his Drambuie and crushed ice. He was unbelievably happy, by and large, although he felt as healthy as he had ever felt, he knew his future, his life was still up in the air. Ever since that day in October when Dr. Jardine had told him his diagnosis was definite and irrefragable. No quarter. Leukemia! Scott never ever said the word out loud and tried never to think of it at all. Dr. Jardine had offered him nothing. No hope. That's where the word hopeless came from! Hope less. Life less of hope. Sans hope. Sans espoir.

Nowhere to go but down. Down. Isabel had been unable to grasp it and had dealt with it, by not dealing with it. "Oh Scott you'll be okay. These guys are wrong ninety percent of the time. "His daughter Carla was the worst. Almost catatonic silence since the news. They'd been so close. Too close really and it was all his fault. It was just the way he was. He loved and worshipped his wife and always would, but his daughter Carla was something else. She was his reason for being. It was why God had made him, he believed, ever since that first time he had heard her. At the Western Memorial Hospital on Premier Drive just hours before she was born, the nurses had greased up Isabel's big tummy and put a strange listening device right on top of her belly button. They'd ordered Scott out of the room during this procedure. A few minutes later he had heard the amplified heart-beat of his unborn daughter. Boom! Boom! Boom! Boom! Boom! God! It was the most overwhelming experience he'd ever had. His eyes glistened even though they were closed tight. "I love you little girl! Come home to your daddy little child, oh you're so welcome in this man's heart my baby! "Scott would never forget the words he had whispered to the empty hospital corridor outside the maternity ward that day. An hour later a nurse with a surgical mask over her face had pushed open the swinging doors of the operating room, walked over to him and put a little, red faced squirming creature in his arms. "Your daughter Mr. Thorne, "was all she'd said. He'd almost been unable to focus on her because he was crying so much. Since then he'd been her shadow. She, his life. There was something about children. He'd always believed that if we could figure it out he'd know and understand the whole point of existence, of why he was put here. There'd be no more war, no more hatred, no malice of any kind, because in the child was the yet, unspoiled human, and the instructions for how to be the perfect race; the one built in God's own image, were in there somewhere and man had not yet figured out what it was. Scott had always known and believed THE ANSWER was in the child, somewhere. He and Carla had grown together. Come to wonder together and everything she had discovered about the world, Scott had discovered. And it was all good. So much fun and laughter and they shared as much of it as they could with Isabel, even though she wasn't onc. Onc of thcm. That special, special kind. A kind they never even spoke about, just always knew existed and that they were two. Special Persons Always Helping. S. P. A. H. That's what he used to call her or Old C. Come on Old C. Let's put the dishes away, he'd say. She'd answer, okay Old Stocking. She's heard him say that was what his grandfather used to call him when he was a child on Bell Island. She'd say stocking like "Thtocking" because of the slight lisp she'd had as a child. It went away as she got older and he and Isabel had clearly and carefully articulated each and every sibilant they uttered. "Okay Old Sssssssstocking!" So when he finally found the nerve to explain to her his illness, it was as if he had suddenly told her that every other thing he'd ever told her was now a lie and to be ignored. The shock on her face was nearly baroque. As if she'd put it there on a whim. All she managed to get out was

"You forgot to tell me that this could ever happen Old Collar." He had been jolted by the t-sucking sibilants in her voice. She'd said, "thith". Then, in a trancelike state she got up and went to her room. All that day he could hear the little music box piano he'd given her for her fifth birthday playing Beethoven's Pathetique, over and over and over. All day and all night.

His Drambuie was warm and the ice melted. He looked at his friends dancing, talking at the tables. Some were hugging, dazed by the evening and incapable of speech. Unable to make a point. A few at the bar were silent. Eating peanuts from a small dish, doodling on a napkin. In the middle of the floor his wife was dancing with his best friend Bruce. They were in a trance too. It was as if they were now all reluctant to let the century and the last 999 years out of their hands, as if they could do anything to stop it. Scott knew he'd have to do something soon to get the party going again. The memory of his hope flooded his mind with sudden joy. There was splendour in the way his face lit up. It was as if a flashbulb had gone off in the midst of all that pseudo-gloom. He looked around and inhaled the sights like a man who'd been underwater too long and had just burst through to the surface. Now his eyes were caressed by the candles as they burned on their tiny tables, wall sconces or in their wrought iron stands, fluttering like burning butterfly wings in tiny crystal holders, smoking and softening the light through the glass. The smells intoxicated him in ways that weren't physical. The long oak tables were laden with huge roasts of turkey, beef, hams, caribou and moose, lobster, crab, hot rum puddings, spicy cinnamon sangrias, and trays full of ice holding up bottles of Bell's Twelve Year Old Scotch. "Only a pagan would drink Bell's warm," Old Sharky Davis used to say on night shift at the mill. The music of this night was the sound of his friends and loved ones, old comrades, even a few old enemies who had gotten together for this one last night of the 1990s. Scott looked down at his own candle sputtering away in a tiny wooden gourd he'd found in an antique shop in Brigus. He said a small prayer as his eyes blurred the pretty flame. He prayed that his hope would be warranted. That Dr. Hamilton Brougham, quack geneticist, according to some, would be right this one time at least. The old researcher had been kicked out of the medical profession a long time ago by his peers in the Canadian Medical Association because of charges that he had experimented with live humans. Actually he had, but they had all come to him and they had all been dying of one incurable disease or another. Since they were dying anyway he had figured the risk was worth it. Unfortunately they had all died anyway and one of them had broken the deal that no one was to know of the injection Dr. Brougham had given them, even if it worked. He'd been hauled before the Board of Directors of the Association and lost his license to practise. Scott had gone to him when the old doctor himself had been near death from old age. He'd told the man of his own illness and begged him to try his serum on him. The old man had refused at first, but Scott kept on trying to persuade him. Suddenly one day the old quack had called Scott and said he'd changed his mind. Scott never did find out that Carla had visited Dr. Brougham, identified herself and then sat in front of him and cried for two hours. She hadn't said a word. Even when he went back to the old man's residence Brougham wouldn't administer the serum. He'd simply told Scott that if anybody were ever to break into his house some night searching for drugs and took that vial of blue liquid there on his desk and injected it into his arm every eight hours for two days, thinking it was some kind of soporific or hallucinogenic, and was then suddenly disappointed that it wasn't that kind of drug, well, it wouldn't really be his responsibility. "Now would it Mr. Thorne?"

Later that night Scott started the injections and two days later gave himself the last one. That was two weeks ago. Scott hadn't noticed anything at first. But in the last few days he had started feeling really good, really healthy and he had run a ten miler this morning, in the hills, and had found it profoundly easy. Also, he had run it in fifty-seven minutes. That was two minutes faster than he had run it when he was the star of the Track & Field Team in high school!

Yep. He was very, very happy that evening. Suddenly he jumped to his feet and climbed up on his chair. "Hey!" He shouted. "Who died? "People stopped what they were doing, looking embarrassed. Scott burst out laughing, started clapping his hands and began to sing," Here we go loop de loop, here we go loop-de-lite, here we go loop de loop onnnnnn a Saturday Night". They joined in. They started clapping. They started singing. They started laughing. They remembered the old song, a favourite of most of them from way back. They smiled and grinned. They started hugging each other as they sang. They kept on laughing and then crying and then laughing. They did that all evening until the year Two Thousand came. They sang Auld Lang Syne for an hour. In a huge circle. Everybody there hugged everybody else over and over. Happy New Year! They said to each other. Happy New Millennium! Happy New World! Scott and Isabel and Carla hugged each other all together. Happy New Life! He shouted to them both and he was very very happy and made them smile.

"I could go on like this forever!" He shouted to them and to his friends and to old All Hallows Hall on Humber Road. And to the known Universe and Creation. "Forever and ever and ever".

And then, he did.

CHAPTER TWO

THARG'S GIANT SPACE-SHIP Lapstrake, "Me dory" he sometimes called it, skipjacked anyway. But he was in deep metal-drag and so he was unaware of it and therefore didn't get sick. Byter had calculated the distance to Credo II and concluded skipjack cruise was called for in order to get there in acceptable time limits. There was a reward waiting there for Tharg for his successful kill, the maverick Scaderk. While he slept he had the nightmare. He was lying on the stony surface of some grey planet, completely alone, perfectly alive, conscious, and utterly incapable of motion. In his dream he'd been there for centuries. All he could do was, in his mind, pray. He prayed for death. He prayed to all the known Gods and to any others that might exist, that he hadn't heard of. None answered and 'he just lay there, silent, motionless, staring up at a grey, empty sky. His mind screamed. Nothing ever changed. He just lay there unmoving, idle, forever.

Then a strange thing happened. He had another dream. It was about God too, and this time, God seemed to be there, sort of. In the dream Tharg met God. Dates, places and events in the dream were very clear, but puzzling. It seemed to go like these . . . Nineteen hundred years after he didn't die (In the dream) Tharg, the atheist, met . . . God! The year 3899 A. D. He had landed on an abandoned Satellite Meteor Station in the Bootes Helix Field. He knew of its existence because 328 years earlier he had nearly collided with it while fleeing a hallucinogenic nightmare that had come after he'd mistakenly eaten South Florian sand hair. He thought he was eating Vegenic Spagh purchased earlier, somewhere. It gave him horrific hallucinations unfortunately, while he was navigating manually, as he often did, to stay sharp. During one particularly intense "vision", microscopic eagles with diamond talons were trying to rip their way into his eyeballs. Naturally, he preferred that this didn't happen so he kept his eyes closed as Lapstrake hurtled through space at vivid rake 98. 9888 . . . . 69th degreeum. A part of his mental reflex made him try to hit the tricontrahedralizer to stabilize no matter what they encountered, but the thought faded before his fingers made contact with the controls. For some insane reason, an old verse of Scripture came unbidden to him and floated around, in his fever to escape the ripping claws. It was the same verse that haunted his waking day dreams at times when he least expected it. Ripping through the galaxy, trying to outrun non-existent eaglets, ever before his Spalling-blue eyes, he heard the verse pounding through his brain like an English kindergarten pupil . . . "Yet a little sleep, a little slumber, a little folding of the hands to sleep." "Oh God," Tharg screamed "Help me! Make them go away!"

Afterwards he was never absolutely certain if he had heard or not, an infinitely still, small voice whisper somewhere in his consciousness, "Get thee hence." He thought he had but was not sure at all. One thing he did know with perfect certainty was that suddenly he was in control of his boat and faculties. Cognition and awareness returned abruptly and as it did his hand blurred to the tricon and engaged. He looked into his exterior screen monitor just in time to see, filling up the Navig-Screen, the Bootes Helix Field Satellite. "Avoid!" He screamed at the Byter (His computer) and Lapstrake lanced tangentially away from the derelict in Blur accelerant. Tharg had taught himself long ago never to indulge in relief after near-misses. "Feel her up Byter, "he ordered, and vast systems of artificial intelligences began a perfect inventory of the Satellite. It found lots of oxidized equipment and tanks full of Faslimion water in seal. Byter recorded it as Tharg staggered to the shower canyons to try and wash away the nightmare and his drugged and painful headache, and figure out what had happened. So, here it was 3899 A. D. and Tharg found himself once again in the same space and according to Byter desperately in need of toning in the wingfan peripherals. He had nothing in his holds that could do the trick so he queried Byter. Response was a reminder of the old satellite at Bootes Helix. "Find and form orbit. He took a Lancer Space Bike, vaguely designed after Belinda, to the landing flats amid the debris of the old floating station. He slipped into his Glenn coveralls and stepped out onto the rusting deck. A Noix melange light tube in his hand, he began to explore. He knew the water tanks were located in the Centre Second of the Three Concentric tubes that formed the station. He flashed his Noix into each room and cubicle he encountered as he walked around the rings. The place smelled like Earth seaweed. He found little of interest in any of the spaces that were filled with brown and grey metal dust as if some great metallic creature had coughed ages into the emptiness. No life form signatures-humanoid or otherwise-and space rust was everywhere, deep and thick. As well there was some kind of metallic fungi clinging to the uprights in places. Everything was dismal, colourless, a mauzy gray ancestors would have said 1900 years ago in the fishing villages of Terra Nova, his home, on Earth.

In one of the larger chambers he saw, or thought he saw, light energies. He entered carefully. His fuzzy beam walking the uprights and corners, all over the detritus of what must have been some kind of communications centre. He could see bits of fibre optic lace and spherical diamond tubing hanging off utterly rusted banks and racks of electroprobic equipment set along the walls, like artificial willow trees. He jumped so high he dented his Lancer cap on the ceiling and had completed forty-seven sets of sword strategy defense and attack Kata forms before he even had a chance to shout out "Catspit!!!" A vaguely familiar voice had whispered in the gloom, over near the willows" 'It's me, "in perfect equanimity and poise. "Hello! Who's that?" Tharg rasped out in his most threatening posture, "Speak and ID. Now! The voice, "It's me." in an inflection, up on the "me as if to say . . ." You know, me! "As if Tharg should immediately identify. Tharg had his sword out, the Noix light rammed under his Cap over an ear, a Runic short dagger in his left hand and an ululate grenade gripped between his teeth. Don't move or I'll shred and mincemeat you. Where are you and Who are you? I'm losing patience." "Scott. It's me. God. I'm over here to your left under the big willow."

"God who and how do you know my name and that's not a willow. Speak!"

"It's God and you were thinking it looked like a willow."

"God who? Bill God? Ramone God? Aspur-Garnian God? Who? How do you know what I was thinking? You're near death now! The truth now! And come out so I can see you. Now!"

"Scott. Scott! Tsk tsk. It's me God. Thee God. You know . . . now I lay me down to sleep, blah, blah, blah. Me. God."

The swordsman was speechless, mystified, in untred waters here. "I can't see you there in shadow. Come out or you'll be sucking this u-grenade down your throat and then you'll be the late God or whoever you think you are. Come out now boy!" Tharg's voice had a slight tremble, which was absurd since he feared nothing known and could not die and even if he could, he'd welcome it. So he found his very palpable timidity in this instance very odd.

From out of the darkened corner came, "Scott Robert Thorne, it's me. You know that. Me. Scott remembers. Go back. Think . . . yet a little sleep, yet a little slumber, yet a little folding of . . ."

"Stop!" How are you, who are you, how do you know that? How could you know that verse? No one knows that verse only me-Tharg! Okay bucko you had your chance!" He tossed the u-Grenade into the corner. Nothing happened.

"It's me, Scottie, God. God." This time the voice was filled with compassion and empathy. Tharg was sobbing. Afraid, like a child.

"Go away. "He whispered. "'way."

After a while, breathing heavily, Scry rasped out in a voice like a little boy, a frightened little boy encountering an invincible bully in the school yard, "Casper God? Waylon? Gordie? Ufullect? Lltript? "He was weeping quietly.

For a while there was silence, except for the cloud-like sound rust makes just lying around, settling on floors, shelves, old satellite stations and around human legs standing in it, immobile, frozen in fear. Tharg sniffed every now and then. Then he said in a voice like a half-round bastard file over a glass edge "I've always liked what you did for Daniel. I hate lions.' Silence. "Sniff." Rust. Tharg. That wasn't very nice what you did to Abraham. That kid didn't do anything to you. Silence. Something shuffling around in the corner under the willow. Tharg instinctively, autonomically poised for battle. "Sniff." "Could I ask you a question?" Silence. "Not if it's about Mary Magdalene and my Son." "Uh. Oh no it's about catspit! That's disgusting about Him and Mary Magdalene. I never ever . . . "I know, but some people have dirty minds." "Sniff." "I just wanted to know about Jonathan and David actually. You know. Were they you know?" "What?" "You know stop it boys Robin's the boss." "Oh. No. They were never, no. Not them.' Suddenly there was a noise and movement from the corner as if something had been knocked over. Tharg jumped. Another u-Grenade in his upraised, cocked fist. "Don't move! Move not! Don't breathe whoever you are! I'll cut you from nave to chap, creature! I mean chap to nave. Whatever! Move and I'll tear out your guts!" Silence. "So. You're not religious . . ." "Funny. Look, just tell me who you really are and I'll let you go. I'll even help you. I'm Tharg-Swordsman. You've heard of me? I won't hurt you I promise. I . . ." "You won't hurt me! That's funny. How's your hull Tharg?" "What's my hull got to do with anything? What hull do you mean? Are we breaking up?" "No. I meant Lapstrake. "You let me worry about Lapstrake and you worry about you. You worry about whether or not you want to leave here in one piece or in several pieces, perhaps a smorgasbord of pieces. Anyway stay put. I'm getting water and leaving. Do what you want whoever you are. Just don't get in my way." "How's your hull Scottie?" Look! Don't concern yourself with my ship. Concern yourself with how you're going to eat your next breakfast through your Adam's apple since your head may very well be AWOL! Now tell me this for the last time, Who the Hell are you?" "Wrong vertical. I'm up. Hell is down. Tsk tsk. That's elementary. You need more catechism Scottie. Bad form old cock. "Old . . . ! Hey! Are you a Newfoundlander? I scanned somewhere they used that phrase?" "God no! Ooops. I mean gosh no. The Newfoundlanders died out with the codfish didn't they?

"WRONG! I'm a Newfoundlander and proud of it and I ain't died out am I?" "Not yet." "What's that supposed to mean? Hey! Are you an Endurion by any chance? If you are your nine hundred years are about to end sport" "Wrong again. How's your hull Tharg? Cleaned it lately? Are lovers glad?" "Black Nova!" What do you mean by that? Why did you say that? Who are you? Who are you? What do you want? How'd you get here anyway?" "Sometimes I like to be alone too Scott. You should understand that. Or to be more true to the genesis of that word, all one." "Don't get deep on me mister. Just tell me who you are and I'll let you play with my sword collection ok? What do you want?" "I want everyone, of course. Don't you read?" Silence. "Okay. I'm outta here. Follow me at your peril knave." As he was backing out of the room Tharg heard the voice one last time. "Keep your hull clean Thorne. You never know when it will mean the difference between Death and Life." Tharg backed out. "You mean Life and Death ninny, "he thought to himself. He went along the corridor to the tanks. Unstrapped three and left. He boarded the Lancer and returned to his ship. He jackknifed out of orbit so fast all the glass in his sword room shattered. He was even tempted to skipjack, but knew his head couldn't take that speed right now. And besides he didn't need to get to another constellation, just out of the district! Goodbye Bootes Helix Field!

Weird dream.

Tharg was afraid. He was never afraid. But now, he was. Things he didn't understand scared him bad. "Maybe I will skipjack. The words of the Cormorant King still bothered him. God hadn't known anything. Just guesses. Tharg wasn't afraid of God. He was afraid of being followed, but not afraid of God. No.

Never.

CHAPTER THREE

EIGHTY-TWO YEAR OLD Scott Robert Thorne looked down at the headstone. He read the inscription:

For, lo, the winter is past, The rain is over and gone;

The flowers appear on the Earth:

The time of the singing of the birds,

Is come.

Carla had always loved the Song of Solomon. That was her favourite Bible verse. He hoped it gave her peace wherever she was now. Her body was seventy-two inches under the Earth at his feet. Her two sons and three grandchildren stood nearby, sniffling. Every now and then they'd glance over at him, their disgust undisguised. Although he was now eighty-two years old, he hadn't aged a day since Dr. Brougham had given him that vial of blue liquid and he'd injected the stuff into his upper arm. In fact, he was lean, tanned, extremely fit. He didn't look a day over twenty-five. That's the estimate most people made of his age. This morning he had run ten miles in forty-nine minutes. His beloved daughter, his treasure Carla, had died of a brain haemorrhage. Her family doctor, Craig Froude, said it had been quick and painless. She died in her sleep. It was a shock to everyone though, because she'd always been so healthy, walking daily, vegetarian diet, no caffeine, she hardly ever had a drink and she had never smoked. Thorne was dazed by grief. He'd loved her with all his might. As she had said to him once when she was a child . . . "Dad, there's not one speck of my heart that doesn't love you!" All her sayings and habits and little idiosyncrasies came back in heart-crushing knocks. Most of all it was her own love for him that had enslaved his heart. She just loved him all her life, an unqualified dedication. He still had all her notes and letters to him in an old crate at home. All her dolls and toys. All her report, cards, diplomas, her degrees, medical reports. He'd saved everything. Cripes he still had her pacifier somewhere! They'd been good pals. Now she lay in the earth, sleeping for God knows how long. He wasn't a religious man so he didn't really have any theories about that. In fact he had often claimed God wasn't a religious man either. That really bugged some of his church-going acquaintances and relatives." Oh! Carla I miss you little one." He wished he was in the ground by her side, protecting her, comforting her. She'd been so helpful to him in the insanity of the years that had followed his recovery from leukemia and the consequent medical miracle that had come. He had stopped aging! Late in January, 2000, he had gone back to Dr. Jardine. The doctor man had examined him, did a series of tests to check the advance of his disease and was stunned when he could find no trace of it whatsoever. He rechecked all the earlier diagnostic results to see if error had been made. He could find none. Scott broke down and told him about Brougham. He tried to explain to Dr. Jardine, Dr. Brougham's theory of Theurgies Genetic Manipulation, TGM. The scion of Thorne's genetic cell had been linked to the moribund parts of another cell in a saddle graft. Thereby the undiseased cells of human genetics that never age are linked forever, much the way chemical units are attached to a molecular chain. The pure, untainted molecules thus enjoyed illicit gain by grafting. There was no rejection as in graft-versus host, related to the bodily condition that results when cells from a tissue or organ transplant mount an immunological attack against the cells in tissues of the host. Brougham had tried all kinds Of Scion-stock grafting of cells not realizing that some existed in the genetic labyrinth that never age and with death simply become genetic detritus. Brougham had hooked these up to the auto-immune system which fights off all disease, even the effects of aging and Thorne's clock had stopped. Brougham had never been able to duplicate this cute genetic trick because he had not been aware of the genes in humankind that did not age. He had always believed that he had linked already dying cells to healthy cells and gained their immune capabilites to overwhelm the bad genes.

In the horrific frenzy of media coverage that eventually came about when it was proved beyond doubt that Scott Robert Thorne was not getting older, Brougham was not a player. He had died, but not before he realized he had at least killed off Scott's fatal illness. But he had left behind no coherent body of scientific research on paper because he'd always relied so heavily on his photographic memory. The most valuable piece of scientific knowledge for the medical world was Scott's own recollection of Brougham's explanation of the contents of the blue vial and what he'd hoped it would do. Scott had a formidable memory himself and could recount each word Brougham had used to explain, unfortunately at the time he had not understood a word of it and had asked no questions. He was afraid to probe too much because he didn't want to hear anything negative. But what he could remember were Brougham's exact words. The scientific community clung to that, but of course, they wanted more.

They wanted Scott.

So his life became bizarre and ugly. Although he'd literally discovered the fountain of youth and was quickly becoming the most healthy human in history, he'd also lost all control over his own affairs. As time went by and he hadn't aged the press got hold of it and started writing stories about him, showing pictures of him then and now. It was evident the man was not getting any older. Suddenly the Federal government wanted to examine him. Under a specially legislated Act of the Department of Health Scott Robert Thorne actually became public property. At first the government had offered him permanent Federal employment as a research project of the Federal Eugenics Program. All Scott had to do was let them take blood samples, tissue samples, stools, urine and bone marrow samples as they wished, and let them record and track his day to day physical status. That's all, and he would be guaranteed employment for life and special federal government treatment forever, or at least until they found out how to duplicate Brougham's intervention. The government even built a special home for him on a small peninsula in Bay of Islands, not far from Corner Brook where they put their team of scientists and researchers from every known discipline, medical, psychological, psychiatric, ethical, sociological and on and on. At first Scott didn't mind a short-term study of his makeup, even a year or two and he liked the little island. His wife and daughter were there and it wasn't so bad, although heavy security kept most visitors away. After a while though, the combined efforts of some of the world's best minds failed to unlock the genetic key that made him different. He decided he wanted to get back to his own life, live in obscurity, for his family's sake and his own. He had enjoyed working in the lab, testing paper for Bowater's Pulp and Paper in Corner Brook. So when he tried to put in his notice he'd been told that for the sake of the future of the human race, he could not leave until they had figured him out. He was told he was selfish. A three year legal battle began with his lawyers arguing his constitutional rights had been violated. His right to freedom, free speech, the pursuit of happiness. The other side argued that the fate of the human race was at risk if Thorne was allowed to go free. The thing ended up in a sensational court trial with the best legal minds of Earth battling it out. In the end, with public opinion heavily against him and his selfish arrogance, he lost and the new

Federal Health Act was enacted. He was now owned outright by the state. To make matters worse, right in the middle of the trial an ugly and very strange incident had thrown a wrench into Thorne's case and his life. A religious fanatic shouting "The Lord giveth and the Lord taketh away!" had shot him right in the heart outside the courtroom. He was pronounced dead on arrival at the hospital and the world went into shock. His wife had a nervous breakdown and had to be taken away. His daughter waited patiently outside intensive care at the hospital refusing to believe he was dead. "Scry Tharg cannot die. He's my dad," she told the surgeons and other staff. Scry Tharg was her version of his name Scott Robert Thorne when she was just learning to talk and couldn't pronounce things properly. She'd often called him that as a term of secret endearment as she got older. He'd told her about it on her eleventh birthday. So, as she sat outside the ER unit at Western Memorial Hospital while the best physicians and surgeons in the world worked on her dad, she sat there, holding her little notebook with his picture laminated on the inside cover and said to herself over and over and over "Scry Tharg. Scry Tharg. Scry Tharg. I love you. I love you." Sometimes she'd say, "I luh you! "The way she'd her her best friend, Xue Ping, a Chinese neighbour say to her family. "I luh you Scly Tharg!" Don't die daddy. Don't die. You promised daddy you'd never leave me. Scry Tharg. Scry Tharg . . .

While the government medical team waited the four hours it took for the world's most famous coroner to fly in from Boston via Toronto, the family gathered in the little church in the basement of St. Henry's School where Scott had been confirmed and received his First Holy Communion. He'd been brought up a Catholic but somewhere along the line he had found the dogma, the icons, the action of the clergy absurd. When he had been confirmed, the Bishop had spoken of the poor of the world and of the sacrifices needed to help them. Then he tapped each kneeling confirmation candidate on the cheek to make them a little soldier for Christ and then they, each in turn, had kissed his ring. "That ring was big enough to choke a buffalo." Scott had mentioned later to his daddy. He'd been sent to bed without his supper for that remark. Although later, his mother had sneaked a roast beef sandwich in to his room to him. "That's big enough to choke a buffalo isn't it?" she'd remarked to him as she handed him the sandwich and a cup of hot tea. They smiled at each other. "Don't tell your father or he'll kill me? "she whispered as she left. Scott's Irish family was heavily into hyperbole. His father was strict, but he wouldn't harm a worm, and besides Scott knew that his mother was the real boss of the house no matter how much his father strutted around the house talking about sinners, the economy and the good Bishop. So when Carla, his parents and a few aunts, uncles and close family friends gathered to pray a Novena to St. Jude, Patron Saint of Hopeless Cases, they were a bit startled when, down at the back of the church, in the evening shadows they heard Scott saying the loudest AMEN! Two of his aunts fainted and Uncle Bert, a religious fanatic, had thrown a tray of Holy Water at Scott and run out of the church. Carla simply walked towards him and said . . ." Well Scry Tharg what have you got to say for yourself scaring the hell out of us. Eh? "News of his remarkable recovery rocked the globe. Scott had simply gained consciousness in the darkened Emergency Room, yawned, got up, found a coat to put on and strolled over to the door where he'd overheard security people talking about the freak's poor family praying their guts out down at St. Henry's. Since the trauma unit is on the ground floor, Scott had simply climbed out of a window and run down over the hill to the church.

After that everything else went downhill too. He was arrested and contained under powers given the authorities by the new Health Act and of course, for reasons of not, national, but world security. They put him into a special quarantine facility somewhere in southern Ontario. His family was out. They could visit him periodically, about once a month, but that was it. Since he wasn't popular with the public., who still believed he was a selfish freak, hardly anyone objected to his incarceration. His wife had been committed to a home for special care, a "Nut House" Carla called it, because she had broken down completely, unable to deal with the unreal world her husband had "caused" by interfering in God's will. That was her way of scolding Scott for taking Dr. Brougham's evil medicine. Carla refused utterly to accept her father's new life as a permanent guinea pig and she decided to get him out of it. It wasn't going to be easy she knew, now that the world had discovered he might actually be indestructible or unendable as Xue Ping had opined. This possibility really bothered the heads of certain other Nations, especially the Russians and the Chinese. They figured that any all-out military confrontation they might have with the Western countries might prove to be a pointless endeavour since there would always be, at least one westerner, Scott Thorne, alive, after it was all over. That gave western nations an advantage they did not like one bit. Why they were concerned over one man's existence, even if everyone else was dead, was never fully explained, but could be grasped in terms of the old boys ancient game of one-up-manship, according to Carla. Anyway the Federal government knew of the concerns other nations had about their special citizen, and security at the facility of his containment reflected this reality. That made it tough for Scott and Carla as they wrestled with the problem of his escape from insanity. Ultimately the establishment itself was responsible for setting him free, although it hadn't been part of the plan. One of the series of tests they had scheduled for him included treating him with extremely toxic viruses, in other words, injecting him or otherwise exposing him to diseases and other fatal elements that killed everybody else. Nice people. A particularly virulent version of one ancient plague that had been developed in the Center for Disease Control in Atlanta, Georgia was due to be tried on him a week before Carla's next visit. The technician responsible for the vial of plague, Carson Wheeler, had been hooked on codeine for a year now, and still wasn't sure of its powers. His job at the research facility was a serious source of depression for him because he and everybody else there, were under such constant scrutiny from security. He knew and all the others knew, that even when they were off base, they were under constant security watch. They were followed, tailed, bugged and Buddha knows what else, at all times. They weren't allowed to drink alcohol or indulge in any other potential inebriants. Carson had discovered years before, however, that a handful of legally purchased acetominophen enhanced with codeine phosphate and caffeine could give you quite a little "boost" of happy happy. Since you could buy it over the counter at any drugstore he did just that, explaining to the druggist that it was the only thing that could help his migraines. So he'd buy a generic version of it, 200 pills at a time. Usually he'd take five or six at a time and feel a nice little buzz for hours. It even helped him sleep, something he'd had a problem with for years. Unfortunately on the day of the experiment with the plague specimen, he'd felt so dreary that he had taken eleven pills at once. The first six didn't seem to have kicked in quick enough to suit him, so he downed another five. While he was in the quarantine care unit transferring the specimen from the tube to a hypodermic needle he became so groggy from the codeine that after the hypodermic needle had been filled, he accidentally pressed the plunger and a minute quantity of the specimen was sprayed out into the air. He was so spaced out he did not notice what he'd done. A few days later almost everyone at the facility was showing early signs of the disease. It was impossible to hide the evidence of this from staff at the facility who were all very bright people to begin with, especially the scientists and their technicians, all of whom were trained observers. One of the technicians figured out almost as soon as the symptons started showing up and told his colleagues. By that time, however, security had been told that no one was to leave the base under any circumstances. Full force was sanctioned. The technicians freaked, and, being smart little persons that they were, concocted a fast acting knockout gas for the nasty little military guys who were holding them against their will. Well, chaos ensued when they started spraying it around. The security force started firing at them, the researchers kept spraying their little gas bomb, protected themselves by face masks, but not from flying bullets. After about twelve minutes of total anarchy everyone at the facility was either shot to death, dying from bullet wounds or unconscious anyway because of the fast-acting soporific spray. Everyone except Scott. He'd seen some of the incident on security screens in the main hall outside his suite of rooms. He'd heard the rest and figured it out quickly. He took his leave of the place as quietly as he could, not knowing for sure if all security was out of action. Before he left he took a mask and a bagful of quarantine disinfectant used to kill contaminants in the field. He'd been told earlier that even though he was immune to all the diseases they were trying on him, he probably carried enough of the germs on him at any given time to kill a small town. When he got about a mile away from the remote security site he took the disinfectants out and doused himself thoroughly several times. He knew the chemicals were extremely toxic to any kind of mite or germ, but he intended to avoid any human contact for a few days, dousing himself daily with the disinfectant until he was satisifed he posed no danger. He had been told soldiers in the field needed only one application to be sure they were clean, but Scott wanted to take no chances. "Scry Tharg is coming home baby. "He said to himself. A few weeks later he managed to slip over the Canadian border into upstate New York. He and Carla had made arrangements long before that if he ever managed to escape they would make no contact for at least a year, or until they were critically certain they couldn't be tracked. The only concession to her concern was to send her a small book of E. E. Cummings poems and signed the inside cover . . . Love Aunt Eulaly. He sent the book to her care of her best friend Dorothy Christopher. She would simply tell Carla at the first convenient time, probably treading water in the middle of the local pool, that she had received a book of E. E. Cumming's from her Aunt Eulaly. Carla would then know Scott was fine and would contact her later. Unfortnately it took him two and a half years before he could arrange to get together with her.

CHAPTER FOUR

AFTER CARLA'S DEATH Scott became deeply depressed. Aspects of their life together haunted him daily. He could hardly bear to go out on evenings when the sky was clear and the moon and stars vivid across the deep canyons of the night. He and Carla had often camped out under the stars in the little campground up on Lady Slipper Road. They'd trout and swim and then, sit around a campfire at night and make up stories about each star, each constellation. Isabel, his wife joined them sometimes but wasn't really a big fan of the outdoors. She was a creature of comfort, although she enjoyed being with her two favourite pals sometimes and she loved nothing better than to haul out her old S. S. Stewart guitar and strum away. Scott and Carla would sing all the old hits, especially Bob Dylan, the Beatles, Neil Young, Johnny Cash, J. J. Cale, Dire Straits, Gordon Lightfoot and lots of silly Top 40 jobbies like Yummy, Yummy, Yummy I've Got Love in my Tummy, Little Red Riding Hood, the Monster Mash and so on. They always finished with her rendition of Dylan's Blind Willie McTell. Isabel had a rough, mannish voice that Scott felt was perfect for the song and it was his favourite.

So now Scott tried to avoid beautiful evenings and certain other occasions and places that reminded him of his lost family. Of course, he could still visit his grandchildren and in-laws, but they didn't really feel comfortable around him. The scientific community had finally given up trying to figure out what Dr. Brougham had done to alter Scott's genetic makeup. After years in seclusion, Scott had given himself up simply because he didn't want to risk getting Carla and her family in trouble with the law. He'd hired a Swiss lawyer, who was the best in his field, human rights, and they'd worked out a deal that Scott felt was a good compromise with the world governments and science if they'd go for it. He agreed they could study and poke at him for another year as they wished, in a secure location, near his family; and then, no matter what they found or didn't find, he would be released. Every six months, however, he'd go to the facility for one weekend so that they could check him out and try other tests and new theories, if they felt they were warranted. In return he was guaranteed a very decent salary for life. He had also agreed to turn over his body to science after his death. As well, if he chose to, all his expenses would be paid if he would agree to travel to other countries where members of the scientfic community were anxious to look at him in the flesh. The offer was open from most countries and every now and then he would pick one out and go for a while. He'd stay as a guest of the host country and back-pack throughout the land. Eventually he got around to visiting most of the countries of the world, learning about their cultures first hand. He also discovered he was becoming very good at learning new languages. Scott had always felt he was a people person and not a things person. He wasn't really interested in the accumulation of valuables or riches. He was, however, very interested in people and their lives, their wants and needs, their dreams, their humour. Scott loved a good joke. He collected them and memorized them. "It is good to be merry and wise. It is good to be honest and true." Carla used to say that. She used to collect sayings, thoughts, sometimes opinions. Her favorite opinion was one Scott had related to her from a young girl who was in town to become a nurses's aid. He'd been eating chips and gravy at the Silhouette Restaurant one Friday night during his high school years. The place was blocked. The topic of discussion at the next booth where all the student nurses's aids were sitting, was the assassination of Kennedy. Scott was listening and watching from his booth because one of the girls was a gorgeous brunette. She had the deepest, darkest eyes hed ever seen. Anyway she was sort of leading out in the debate about Kennedy's death. All the girls took part except a shy, little strawberry blond in the corner. It was obvious to Scott she wanted to join in, but couldn't think of anything intelligent to say. Finally after a long lull in the conversation, she took a quick sip of her Keep Cool lime and said, "I don't think they shoulda shot him." The other girls looked at each other trying not to smirk, and the gorgeous doll Scott had been drooling over reached over and patted the blond on the wrist and said, "You're absolutely right Ivy. Nobody deserves to be shot like that." Ivy looked proud, happy, smug. Scott left the restaurant, went outside and doubled over with laughter. From then on every time he was engaged in a dull conversation with his buddie she'd say, "I don't tink they shoulda shot him." For years that became a popular saying in Corner Brook, but only Scott knew where it had come from. Carla loved the story. Even though Carla had been a senior citizen when she died, she would always be Old C to Scott. He was devastated by her death. He knew someday she would die, but he had never prepared for it because it was such a negative notion. He still couldn't believe it. He couldn't. Didn't know how. He had no idea how he was going to keep going now. He didn't want to. Had no desires. No interests. His life was tasteless. A mouthful of dust. Except for memories. He had fantastic memories. His life had been very good, delicious really, in spite of the aberrations. He had come to love certain events in his past and they and their memories had become precious to him. His wife Isabel, had been the only love of his life. Not just the best but the only one. They had met at a Friday night dance in the White House, a former USO club in Corner Brook. The band, the Valiants, was playing House of the Rising Sun. He was drunk. It was his favorite song at the time. He took the microphone from the lead singer, a good friend of his, Terry Artis, and started singing the song himself. He got a standing ovation when he was finished and then got kicked out. Isabel had followed him outside and when the bouncer and everybody else had gone back inside she sat up on a rail on the veranda staring at him. He was sitting on the steps laughing. "I like your voice a lot Thorne." He'd looked up startled. "You sound just like Eric Burden." God! That was about the biggest compliment you could pay a guy who loved the Animals. "Who are you?" he asked. She was dark and cute. Nice legs. "I'm a firefly." "Uh-huh." "Actually I'm a shooting star. "Silence. He stared at her. "Isabel Wass from West Valley Road. Mike Wass's sister. "Mike was the goalie for the local Catholic High school hockey team. "I know Mike. He's a great goalie. Reminds me of Terry Sawchuck. "Ha! He'd go cracked if he heard you say that. He hates Sawchuck. "Oh. Well in that case he's sick." Silence. "Dylan's a Jew ya know." "So? "Indignation.

"Some people don't like Jews, but I, personally love Dylan. "She was swinging her legs. Those, legs. "You're going to fall off if you keep doing that, "he observed. "I love Like a Rolling Stone. "Silence. "I love Blind Willie Mctell. "She had nice hair too. "I never heard of that." "Obviously you don't know Dylan. "Listen here Thorne! I know Dylan better than anyone in Corner Brook including you mister!" "Jees! Calm down will ya. "Real nice hands, long and thin fingers. Cool legs. Silence. Moose Dingwell, the huge doorman at the White House dance came over. "Go away Thorne". "No." "I'll invaginate ya if ya don't".

Moose was not the top student around town but loved learning big words and using them as often as he could t prove he could be the top student around town.

"I'll bleed all over ya Moose".

"Just go away Thorne. You're drunk."

He walked away.

"Well I think I'll go over to the Glynmill Inn for a beer."

"Oh well excuse me. I didn't think you were old enough to get in there."

"I ain't, but me and the bartender's friends. She goes out with a French Canadian guy who works for that company building the new machine at the mill. I talks to him in French. His name's Maurice."

"How come you can speak French?"

"I dunno. I just likes it."

"Oh. Well see ya.

"Yeah. See ya Isabel. Maybe I'll see ya next Friday night at the dance again. "She had a really, really, really nice front.

"Yeah. Maybe. See ya. Thorne.

They got married a year after he started work at Bowater's on Number Six sulphite machine. Reverse truckdriver. Turn left. Go right. They were married at the Columbus Hall. About two hundred people showed up. Mostly his buddies and their wives or girlfriends and parents, and a lot of guys from the mill plus some friends of his older brothers he didn't really know but who liked to drink for free. His best friend Norm got loaded and couldn't drive him and Isabel back to their newly rented apartment so Quill Kilpatrick drove them, a cool guy from the mill who also loved Dylan and who had an IQ of about 160. When they got to the door of the apartment, up over Club 17 Scott got embarrassed and excited and invited Kilpatrick in. Kilpatrick got excited too and didn't know what to do so he came in and they all sat in the little kitchen and drank a few beers. Then Scott and Keith drank more beers. Then they drank more. Then Keith went out to his car, a souped up '63 Plymouth Fury and got a bottle. They all drank more and Keith even made the bride a cocktail, her first. Then she fell asleep. Scott and Keith drank the bottle and then fell asleep. The marriage was not consummated that night but Scottie did learn that Keith was in love with one of his class mates, a girl from Curling who hated Scottie because he was a "Little drunk." Keith said he'd dump her in the morning, even though he had never dated her and was madly in love with her. In the morning Isabel woke up on the chesterfield and saw Scott and Keith asleep on their new bed, which had never been slept in, their arms under their heads, unconscious. Their rented tuxedos would need a great deal of work before they were returned. She started laughing and couldn't stop. She laughed so long and hard that the people in the other apartments above Club 17 started knocking on the wall telling her to shut the f..k up. "So she stopped laughing after a while and then went to her little kitchen and fried a ton of bacon and eggs. Then she made toast and coffee. Then she dragged the two old buddies out to the kitchen, made them sit up and eat. They both had three helpings each, gallons of tea, sugar and Carnation Milk, and then, both of them elegantly slipped outside to the alley and threw up. When they came back she gave them both hot toddies. They sipped slowly for an hour or so and started to come around. She watched them and tried not to laugh again, although she was sorely tempted. She looked at Scottie. He looked like a corpse. "Good morning husband", she said. He looked at her and then ran out and threw up again. She couldn't help it it. She started laughing. After awhile the hot toddies started to get through to Kilpatrick and then he started laughing. Then he went out and bought another bottle. After awhile they were all laughing again.

It was three days after the wedding when the marriage was consummated. In Scott's little yellow Volkswagon on the way back from Dr. Pullen who was treating Scott for acute gastritis. They parked behind the Esso station on Humber Road and made Carla.

That night Scott went to work at the mill driving the reverse-steering power truck on Number Six. At Four o'clock in the morning while thinking of his new bride he drove the truck and eight four-hundred and fifty pound bales of sulphite over the wharf. The truck and sulphite were lost. Scott managed to make it ashore in time to be suspended for three weeks. Those were the only three weeks of his life he never went outside for even five minutes. He found out the headboard on his brand new bed was only made of corrugated plywood and easily breakable.

Thinking back on those days now tore at him. God he'd loved all that life! He'd loved Isabel Wass so much! He'd loved Carla Thorne so much! He'd loved Kilpatrick so much! He even loved Ivy! "Shouldn'ta shot him!" He started to laugh. Then cry. "What am I going to do nowWhat's the point? I'm a freak. Everybody I loved is dead, and there's no grave for me.

He cried for a long time. Days and days. Then he decided to become Scry Tharg. And then, he did.

CHAPTER FIVE

BYTER BEGAN AN adrenalin drip into Tharg's leg as Lapstrake approached the Maison Neux Galaxy. The Inns of Court were there on the planet known as Qua. It was there the swordfighter had to go to collect his reward for the duel with the Scaderk Officer. People used to believe years ago that travel through deep space was a silent affair. But the noise in some parts of the Giant ship was deafening. The Carb Thrusters made the most noise. They used a complicated combination of old-fashioned nuclear furcation energy and the nitric drive System invented by Stith Hansen in 3447. The Black Soot Booster it was called by those in the illicit underground trade of galactic flight systems. So-called because of the implosive centripetal cloud of utterly black energy that hovered around the entire drive-system while it was engaged. The enclosed space holding the device had to have geniculated walls with double furring because of the minute, but horrific vibration attendant with engagement. In the early days of its use many drive system engineers and technicians had been lost to the cloud, which not so much incinerated them, as engulfed or absorbed them into the black. No one had ever survived contact and only one human limb had ever been recovered. Changed completely into what looked like an anthracite carving of a human fist, it had been dropped onto a stateroom deck and crumbled into black ash. There were many other noise emissions on board Lapstrake including Byter itself, one of the largest pieces of artifical intelligence equipment in the known camps. Tharg had paid a colony of planets that he had discovered for it and to have it installed on Venus-of-the-Trades by aliens who had once been humans. They had traded their humanity in order to mutate into slight ephemeral wisps of light and thereby join the newly discovered race of aliens humans called the Cadre. Actually newly announced would be more appropriate, since they had sent a delegation of their peoples to all the major governments in all the constellations. They told each they had decided to make themselves known because of their great interest in articifial intelligence from which their own species, had evolved back in their long bright past. They announced they would not help any of the races improve or advance their systems but could and would offer their knowledge and skills to repair existing equipment. They claimed they could make new any piece of equipment and solve any problems with any software program extant. Their only payment would be that they would be given permission to invite any humans who so wished to become a member of their species through mutation. They promised that these humans would then learn how to and proceed to do the work on any humanoid inteligence systems that needed repair or refit. It was agreed and since then, a mutually acceptable co-existence had evolved, although to date, only one of the Cadre had ever been known to appear at any one time. This led to speculation that there was indeed only one and that was why they needed human volunteers to make more. But the human volunteers, all mutated on Venus-of-the-trades were rarely seen again and only one at a time ever worked on humanoid equipment and that one looked identical to the only known member of the alien race known as the Cadre. Tharg knew their secret but never told.

Other equipment on his great vessel that made noise were the life support systems, his weapons stacks which he kept on idle at all times, a practice that paid off on a number of occasions and Butterfly Creek, Deck Six where he kept a number of specialty items peculiar to his own tastes and which had nothing to do with running a ship. For one thing, Deck Six contained his personal weapons room, the main feature of which was his vast display of working blades. Swords and knives, pikes, bayonets, lances, many swinging weapons such as a Capillet mace and the Brownrigg Craw, a vicious ball at the end of a short vellum-chain and imbedded with tiny nodules that exploded on contact with an opponent. The explosions were contained to a cocoon of five inch diameter, in which, usually everything in reach disintegrated. Tharg didn't use it. He thought it would be cheating to use it in any fight.

In other rooms on Six you'd find his nearly complete collection of recorded music since the 1940s, all fully and faithfully reproduced on optic-disctubes. He had lots of favourites and had heard them all many times, over the centuries. In one small pneumatically sealed cubicle at the end of a long corridor on Six were the remains of Dr. Brougham, the man who had made Tharg immortal. Most of the time Tharg forgets he has him on board. He had at one point wanted to see him ensconced in some great memorial where all the universe could pay him homage as the only being who had ever beaten death. Sometimes Tharg loves Brougham. Sometimes, though he hates him and curses him for turning him into a freak. The corpse was badly deformed even though Tharg had managed to get him out of the cryogenic storage facility before too much damage had been done to the cells. But as a last gesture of scientific passion Brougham had injected himself with a special concoction of genetic material he'd taken from a rare African ant that he believed could genetically alter humans enough to give them tougher, almost indestructible skin, without losing its other properties. A week later shell-like extrusions started appearing on his upper body and neck. They remained until his death and even now after all these centuries, they were still evident on the man's corpse. A sort of badge of honour, Tharg felt, to the man's passionate curiosity.

Besides a vast library, gymnasium, spa, tool room and electronic, mechanical, drive system workshop Tharg had a small room which contained his most prized possession, a 1990 1340 Harley Davidson Fat Boy touring machine. It was in factory condition at all times, silver grey, cold black tires, Tharg cherished the machine. He called it Belinda, a name his uncle on Bell Island had called his motorcycle, a Vincent Black Shadow, and one of the first bikes in the old mining town. Motorcyle riding was just one of the thousand or so skills he had picked up after his various families died on him. He had tried to maintain contact with the great-grandchildren and their children, and their grand-children and on and on of his daughter and her sons. But after a few centuries he found they no longer related to him or had any interest in him whatsover and any genetic resemblance to him or his earlier family had long been bred out through successive generations of marriage and intermarriage. So he'd dedicated his life to learning. He enrolled in the best universities under many pseudonyms and studied many subjects. He became Scott Robert Thrne, Phd. History, Kyle Roy Scott, Phd-Biology, Robert Scott Roberts, Phd. Chemical engineering, Rik Thompson, Phd. Genetics. He became a medical doctor, a philosopher, an aeronautical engineer and fuel specialist with the space programs of several different countries. He studied many subjects including geography, astronomy, astro-physics, marine biology, paleontology, and so on. As well, he mastered trades such as plumbing, car and motorcycle mechanics, marine engine repair, carpentry, electrical and electronic technologies, and the like. He studied every known form of martial art, loved to box, and became a weapons master in all personal weapons and as well, learned to understand, operate and even build and rebuild every other weapon system in existence at the time he was learning, from Claymore mines to nuclear warheads and plastics. He learned most of the extant languages simply because over time, he'd lived with every culture on every corner of the globe and later with the advent of space travel. He was, in other words a true Renaissance man, a classic with one major difference. He was immortal.

CHAPTER SIX

THARG HAD TO wait three days in a small dirty room over the Brock's Head Pub before he could gain an audience with Emminence Va at the Inns of Court on Qua. It had been built for him. He was there to claim his reward for the death of the Scaderk who had had the temerity to crash-land on Qua a while ago, have his vessel repaired and then slaughter the crash crew of Quans who had worked on his ship. His only explanation had been that no one but a Scaderk can see the inside of a Victorial Spacer. The Maison Neuf galaxy held many planets but only those near the Qua had any life forms living on them. Qua itself had nine small, spastically orbiting moons around it, known as the Nine, hence the name of the galaxy. The orbits of the small moons were so unpredictable that travelers who pre-set their flight navigs based on a median of the last known orbits often got a real bad shock when they suddenly found their space craft hurtling along at blur speed heading strait into the center of a Quan moon. That's what had happened to the Scaderk; he hauled off auto-flight just in time to graze the moon and just barely made it to a plain on Qua. Emminence Va had called for

Tharg immediately because the Inns of Court had decreed death as soon as possible, at all cost for the Scad, and only Tharg had the resources to find the Scaderk before he died of old age and was killed by someone other than those carrying out an act of honour on belhalf of Qua. The Quans were known throughout the camps for their legendary system of justice and Emminence Va was so revered by Quans and others alike that he was often referred to as Emminence Solomon. Finally Tharg was called. He walked to the vast rock fortress known as the Anjou, after a place in France on Earth that still held a giant castle known as Chateau Angers and after which the Anjou had been designed. In fact, the Anjou was an almost exact copy, except, instead of being built by the famous black slate of France it had been made of Quan's brittle grey soil, compressed into huge square blocks and other shapes by a system the Quans also used to make their reknown Optic diamonds and gems. It was indestructible. Unlike the great towers of Chateau Anger though, the Anjou featured only four, and each one held an Inn of the Courts. One housed Emminence Va Supreme, who looked after all matters of Quan security and matters of honour, ethics and the like. Emminence Gris was housed in another tower. His demesne was planetary, national and local governments. Emminence Nanc, the only female legalist was in the Ceramic Tower, so named because she had had the entire inside of the vast hall covered in ceramic tiles, each depicting, in miniature graphics, a piece of Qua history involving a decision of the Courts made in her Tower. She was also the mate of Eminnence Va. Her specialty was family law, lands and genetics. The last tower held the home of the Inner Temple, the only court that dealt with strictly religious matters of which the Quans were the most contentious debaters in all the knowns. Tharg had been on Qua several times before he'd been hired to get the Scaderk, and on one occasion just for fun he had told a Quan priest from the Court of Emminence Nanc that he had just heard a new piece of dogma that said the Christian God known as Jehovah had never ever had a choice as to whether or not He could exist. Well naturally this statement made the rounds quickly and before long the most incredible debate in Qua histories had been ignited with one side saying of course, that since God was God He did have a choice. The other side maintained the contrary and on it went. Tharg stayed behind a few weeks thoroughly enjoying the drivel, laughing his heart out. On the day he left, as he was tightening a brake on Belinda, before riding out to his ship, he spoke, once again, to the same young Quan priest and told him he'd heard that indeed God had had a choice, but one of them was not to exist as God, per se. The young priest had started to cry and rushed away, pale and shaken. Tharg had roared off across the plain towards Lapstrake grinning from ear to ear.

Emminence Va, Tharg was surprised to observe, was sitting on his Bench flanked on each side by the other Justices. His wife was smiling at Tharg and with a nod of assent from her husband spoke to Tharg. "You and I must get together someday Swordsoul and discuss the existence of God, don't you think?"

Tharg looked away, a little nervously. "M'am I'm sorry but I have a rule about politics and religion. I never debate them except with an obvious inferior. So far, I haven't had that debate." "Nanc laughed and said to her husband, I too have a reward for Thargsman. She motioned with her hand and a court guard wheeled over to the Swordsman a massive 144 Volume Encyclopaedia entitled, "Gods; Known and Unknown and their Irrelevance to the Krys-God of Quan". Tharg blushed. "There's a very interesting treatment in there Mr. Tharg on the many and various sad fates that have befallen the irreverent, and by the way, not one of those fates, was death, but all were very unpleasant." Tharg glanced up at her long enough to be confused by the look on her face. Smirk or frown he couldn't say. "My great pleasure Madame Justice. I thank you. It shall feature prominently in my library." She interrupted him, "Indeed it will Master Rider and remember, there will be a test next time you return to the Sacred Planet!" Tharg looked extremely uncomfortable and didn't know what else to say. He was just about to make another verbal blunder when Emminence Va stood up. All the other Justices rose to their feet immediately and stood respectively quiet looking at Va. "Scry Tharg you have brought the stone?" Tharg reached into his jacket and brought out the tiny Scaderk amulet and chain worn by all Victorial Guards. He brought it forward and laid it on a small desk before the bench of Emminence Va. The Justice and his colleagues leaned over looking at the object with disgust. Va waved with his hand and his Chief of Security came forward, picked up the amulet, scanned it with a blood-red tube of some kind and put it back down on the bench. He looked at Emminence Va, bowed and spoke. "It is Scaderk Your Worship."

"You commanded me Va? "An ancient voice from the rear of the hall whispered so that they all could hear. Everyone turned. It was Trisk Madam Perigueux, the Holy Weaver. Suddenly everyone in the hall knew what Tharg's reward would be and gasped with shock and envy. Madame Nanc was visibly upset, and although she would never say against a decision of her mate in public, she gave him such a look that he flinched anyway.

He stood up, lay the long wooden box he'd had in his hand on the arm of his chair, opened it and took out the Chain Necklace of Perigueux Optics, the only one in existence. He put it over his head and in place around his neck. "Now with authority of the Inns of Court supported by the vote of accession and emboldened by the Chain of Perigueuex, I declare as law that the reward of Scry Tharg-Swordsman, Master of Lapstrake, Dr. Bladesgore, for fulfilling his contract with the citizens of Quan be the gift of weaving the Optics."

Silence.

Tharg couldn't believe his ears. The ability, the craft of weaving the exquisitely delicate blue strands of Quan optics from the air of Qua was known only to it's discoverer Trisk Madam Perigueux, who some said was as old as Tharg and to Emminence Ghand, the only living retiree of the Inns of Court, the man who had written all the rules and set the codes that had made the Inns the most sought-after legal decision making industry in all the galaxies. It was said that Trisk Madam Perigueuex had been visited by an angel or a God when she was a young virgin and because of her beauty and purity, given the gift, more or less, as inducement to continue her goodness. She had never publicly nor privately acknowledged this, and it had always been rumoured that she and Glhand had been in love, but never loved. He had never married, and she had stayed a virgin, as far as anyone knew. When her gift had become a matter of public knowledge the Inns of Court had met and decreed that she should become a public treasure of Qua and a ward of the state. Since Trisk Perigueuex had come to love the weaving more than anything else, and because the state was going to set her up in her own small house on the high corner of one of the four Towers, she'd agreed. Only on special occasions did she ever weave in public. Anyone watching the sacred event would see only the frail old lady reach into the empty air with her tiny, bony fingers and seemingly stir the air for a minute or two. Gradually, very slowly infinitesimally thin strands of an exquisitely blue fiber appeared in the air above her fingers and took on a shape of her own choosing. Usually people could recognize the object as a reproduction of some great historic hero from the Quan past. When she was finished with her weaving, she'd sit in a chair near the four Justices, for she only weaved in Anjou, and the tiny blue figure would, come to life and go through an intricate mime of its own history, perhaps fighting some great battle, or creating some great law or code or structure. Once she had weaved two figures and when she'd taken her seat, the audience was overwhelmed when the two went through a mime of love-making and produced their own third figure, the last king of Qua, Barry Reickh the very one who had ordered an end to the monarchy, and the establishment of the Inns of Court. Everyone in the audience that day had knelt and bowed before the miniature king. He had seen them all and raised his hand to them in Benediction. The figures always faded after an hour or so. Trisk Madam Perigueuex had long ago stated that the Person from whom she'd learned the weaving had told her that one day she could teach two others, a decision that would be made and decreed by the Emminence Va of the day. "Come Tharg!" she stood by the swordsman's side and took his hand, bringing another gasp of shock even from the Four because it was the first time in her life that she had knowingly touched another being. She hadn't even shaken hands with her old friend Ghand. Tharg was nearly in shock with awe. He looked up at the Va and tried to say . . . "Your Emminence I prefer to claim no reward rather than take your sacred weaving from you in such an unworthy fashion. I am the least worthy in all the known . . ." "Silence good soldier!" It was Nanc. "If you are not worthy, you who make the worlds safe for honour and dignity and integrity, then no one was, is or shall be."

Silence.

Tharg reached down and unstrapped the Blue Charm. He walked forward with the old blade and laid it on the bench. "I would consider it a favor if you kept this most-true blade and hung it on the wall of the Anjou somewhere. It is the blade that delivered your honour." He straightened out and saluted all four. With his hand in the old woman's, he was led out and up to her high tower where she would teach him how to weave the Perigueux Optics. And then, she did.

CHAPTER SEVEN

VULCAN PRISON, THE Cathedral, gored the sky's vapor-red filth. There was so much pollution on Vulcan that even the air over the cities held floating debris, dirt, refuse. The hellish environment below wasn't fit for habitation of any kind and yet there were more than thirty million creatures of every ilk, living there, serving sentences for crimes they might or might not have committed, depending on which political system they come from and who their enemies were. There were at least two million, one hundred and twenty-eight thousand spouses there, male, female, other, whose mates either got bored with them or who had felt they deserved to live in hell. They must have been hated because life on Vulcan was not better than death. There were many cases on record of prisoners who had self-imploded in the court docket as they were sentenced, rather than allow themselves to be put on board the Black Maria with Captain Blax, Master of the prison ship. It is said that implosion destroys body and soul and so the convicted chose, rather than risk even their souls ending up with Blax. Because life on Vulcan, was in many ways, a breeze compared to the horror of incarceration on board the Black Maria, Blax's patrol wagon. The Black Maria was a giant space barge that collected prisoners from all over the galaxies and shipped them to the prison planet. Blax was an alien from the Calder Reeves, that ugly cluster of meteor-like, tiny planets so well known for the horror its inhabitants inflict on each other as their favourite pastime. The ugliest of all the planets there, was The Vragga, and its denizens were the most foul and evil in all the knowns, of the many planets which hire mercenaries from all the other worlds, very often to carry out dirty, illegal missions, only The Vraggans were known not ever to have been hired. They were simply too treacherous. They were too incontinent in their lusts and hatreds. It was well known that prisoners being escorted to the pits of execution on Vragga were often gutted before they ever got there simply because their guards could no longer wait for the pleasure of the cuttings and the tars. There were legends about how the Vraggans got to be like that. The most commonly believed was that when the Christian God had warred in Heaven with the bad angels before He had ever created planets, He had beaten them all by casting them out onto lesser worlds. Satan, for example, it was believed by the religionists had landed on Earth. His brother Vragga had been thrown onto that ugly rock to do what he wanted there. Vragga, the fallen Devil then, had been the first Vraggan and when others of his kind had been kicked out of Heaven and landed there with him, they had formed the first community on Vragga. And they all blamed each other for their hellish lot and acted accordingly, without honor, integrity, or dignity. Hatred and pain-lust their only pleasure and vice. Or so it was believed. Blax, more than anything else, seemed perfect proof of that theory. His thirst for the pain of others had never been sated. It couldn't be but, he kept trying anyway. So when the tender call was made throughout the planets, for someone to operate the Black Maria prison barge that would carry the most dangerous, vile and unpredictable criminals the galaxies would spawn, nobody but Blax had bid on the contract. He had prepared his bid basing it on his estimation that he could guarantee, by and large, fifty to sixty percent delivery success, condition of the prisoners no guarantee, except they'd still technically, alive. His signed contract stated that if the percent ever dropped below fifty more than four consecutive trips it would be broken and his licence revoked. More than once it had gone below fifty percent three consecutive times. On many occasions when he had delivered a fifty-five percentile, fifteen percent had died in the week following delivery. Blax treated all prisoners on board his black monstrosity the same, as ants who, if they got in his way, were crushed, and as lab animals. As soon as he had his full onboard quota and set out for Vulcan, he'd begin his experiments with his live cargo. Drugs, electronics, entomology, parasitic biology and every other kind of vileness was used as scientific equipment, and infrastructure in the lab on board the Maria. He called the lab . . . The Playhouse. One legend that had been born a few years after he started working the Vulcan prison contract was that the air on board the vessel was thick with the souls of the dead looking for live prisoners to inhabit in the hope they could turn the body of the host against Blax for revenge. Blax also had heard this legend and partially believed it. In the event he encountered a prison inmate he believed might be one of these soul-invaders, he used very special care to be horrifically merciless with them in his little lab games. No prisoner ever escaped the attention of the Blax Master. The ones who survived and were ultimately delivered to make up the proper percentages of his quota were said to be far worse off than any dead. Often his prison population was made up of whole families, his fave. These were always saved for the tail end of the trip. First of all, so that they'd start to get the impression that he had compassion for families, and therefore his enjoyment at the sudden realization of their horror was even greater, and also because he usually had to hurry in his punishment of the family unit. No family had ever been included in the fifty-to sixty precent to survive the trip. No child had ever made it either. Children were his special passion. He had a room on board the Black Maria he liked to call the Visitor centre. In it he would put children who were told they were waiting to be re-united with the rest of their familiy. Once seated in the room, the door locked, one wall in the room became a big viewing screen. The feature movie of the day was the recorded torture of that child's family, in full colour and sound. Blax often sat for hours watching the child go insane as he saw his family barbarized. He wasn't a nice person. He was content though, with his career choice. Only one thing could make him happier. A chance to get his hands on Scry Tharg. The swordsman had once actually boarded the Black Maria and freed every prisoner. He'd taken them on board Lapstrake and taken them, well, no one knows where really, although one rumour is that it was to a green planet in Vix quadrant and set them all free. Blax hadn't been happy. He'd tried to gut Tharg with every dirty fighting trick he knew, and in that regard his knowledge was vast but he hadn't scratched the Earthling. Tharg had jettisoned his engines and left him alive but sealed in a self-contained domestic unit in the aft of, the ship. He'd drifted for eleven years before being rescued by a salvage ship from Vragga which had then tried to lay legal claim to the Maria and the prison contract. Blax managed to get them all eventually into his special lab. He'd been able to renew his contract work with the prison authorities because none of the agencies who had filled in while he was lost in deep space had lasted more than two trips. And crime statistics had gone through the Nebula Strata when the dark side had come to realize no matter what happened to them they'd never have to put up with a Blax again. The establishment was glad to have him back. Blax had also been told that Tharg had left the area on a survey mission to chart the borders of the known worlds. So now in the Warden's office of Vulcan prison Blax was meeting Deputy Warden Church Harllan who was telling him a very interesting piece of news. He was telling Blax that a former Captain of the Prison Guards claimed he knew a way to capture Scry Tharg. He knew something about Tharg that nobody else knew that he could use to entice him into an ambush situation where toxic but non-lethal gases would be used to knock out the swordsman for months. Blax had tried to threaten the Deputy Warden with violence and a trip on board the Black Maria if he didn't tell him where he could locate the former Captain of the Prison Guards. It didn't work and instead, Harrlan was demanding a sum of money Blax wasn't even certain existed. Blax had his resources, however. Even though he was not interested in the accumulation of wealth, pain was his only joy, he did know one sure way of raising lots of money. He could easily ransom literally thousands of his prisoners for unheard of figures. He made a deal with Harllan to get the money he asked for. Harllan said something then that nearly made Blax gut him. He told him to hurry because he had three other buyers and whoever came up with the money first would get the deal. Blax sat silently for a few minutes and then took a small video capsule out of his tunic. He laid it on the table and told Harllan to view it when he had the chance. His last words to the Deputy Warden had been, "If I don't get your money to you in time and someone else gets Tharg, I believe that will cause me to become necessarily preoccupied with getting my hands on someone else instead." Then he left. Harllan picked up the video capsule, dropped it on the prison floor and ground it into glass dust with his heel. He knew what it was. A short feature on highlights of a trip to Vulcan from a prisoner's point of view. Oh, he fully intended that Blax would be the one to win the deal for Tharg. He fully intended that Tharg would end up in one of the labs on board the prison barge. But what Blax wouldn't know until it was too late was that Tharg would not be incapacitated. He would only be pretending to be. Harllan knew that Tharg would then finally take care of Blax. Then Harllan could rest easy knowing that his young sister and her husband and child who had been sent to Vulcan on board the Black Maria had been revenged.

Flying back in his shuttle to the prison space bus Blax sat quietly staring down at his gnarled hands. His smile was the stuff of nightmares. He felt good. He knew Harllan would doublecross him and he knew why. His onboard computers kept records of all former prisoners and all their familial conections and relationships of every kind. Blax remembered what held done with Harllan's younger sister. It had been an interesting experiment with a Xrissian cougar and the girl. Poor thing. Just hadn't been in the mood. Blax smiled. He bit his lips so hard his blood was black on his smile. Happy. Happy. Happy. He'd have Tharg. He'd have Harllan. He'd have everything. Life was good. Quite decent he thought.

CHAPTER EIGHT

"THE ABOMINATE! THE abominate!" Xe tzrect! Xe tzrect! "In a vast hall on Endurion, the long-lived Cyclids, by the ten thousands, grunted out the name of the hated one in lavic rage. Xe tzrect!" It was Tharg . . . the abominate. The Xe tzrect. To the Endurion race, the Cyclids, the most long-lived creatures in the worlds, many more than nine hundred Earth years, or an Endurion elctrong, Tharg's longevity was bitter bile. An abominonable stench in their sporil cavities. For all of time they had been the pride of the long lifers. They had outlived all others. All, others. They'd been . . . legend. They had been prided. Feted. Saluted. Known. Honoured and sancted. Blessed by hundreds of years of life. They had been given. They'd enjoyed enormous advantage over their enemies, and also friendly neighbours, of whom there were few. Their gelid metabolism, so slow a chemical and genetic process, such a long cyclidion journey that it gave them long years, and thunders of advantage over all others, and they were very hard to kill. In battle, when wounded, their metabolic reactions were so slow to absorb trauma, an incisive slash for example, that their healing and succouring mechanisms, vastly and ironically, quicker than everyone elses, beat the physical damage to the punch every time. As Bobby Twajc used to say to Tharg on Fortis Ranch . . . "An Endurion, in his death throes, is healthier than a Samyon marathoner at the starting lists!" Tharg laughed and pointed out their only weakness . . . "Hit them in the mandible sac, center of their healing mechanism, and the race between life and death is over, because you've knocked out that extraordinary healer." But he always felt the sadness that comes with the notion of the death of the magnificent life essence of an Endurion Cyclid.

In the Saerl Space Arena on Endurion the sea of froth and rage for Tharg, the Immortal, went on. His usurpation of the pride of longevity from the Cyclids was as egregious to them as pedicide was to humans, or fecta mangils, the ingestion of human waste, practised by Convectors on Paris 932. The humanoid form of the Cyclids hid their un-Earthly features until close-up. They had no ears, a long strip of seam-like lip was their sight organ and their oral cavity was a stiff vertical, fleshy engrowth, much like a terran caterpillar.

Although it never actually opened, it took on many shapes and sizes during communication. When they were enraged, a rarity itself, almost as rare as an Endurion gathering of more than three, forbidden by the Trsl dogma, their oral organ, in Endurion sounding like, thesplistli, took over the entire skull surface, at points of peak frenzy and rage. They had a torso, limbs, arms, leg trunks much like humans, but covered all over in a pale, pink, bony surface, with keratosis evident throughout. Their hand metaphorics were three long fingers, more like the larger cartilage of a lobster claw, but leathery. They stood erect on a splayed triptic, two in front, one on the side. Their only weapon, a device that resembled a geiger counter, a stick with a flat plate at the end, all black metallic, no markings, was a metab-projector. It was capable of projecting the wielders own metabolic force into an opponent, rendering same into slow-motion death that often took weeks, sometimes months. The Cyclids never stayed, once it started and that was usually, instantaneously. They could not stay to witness the death of another because death to them was as heinous as any sacrilege. It was necessary, yes, but too odious to share space, time or thought with. "The abominate! The abominate!" The Cyclids sent the sound of their disgust and rage out in waves of repeating syllables. "Xe tzrect!" To a human it would have sounded like a small wave on a lonely beach. To the genetically subdued Endurion it was a cacaphony of screaming and loathing. Above the assembly Spar Tr suddenly appeared in his chariot of Cyclid mandarins. They flew forward, upright, with the platform of Corian bone, shining like Purf oil, on their shoulders. Soundless, the spectacle ceased motion above the gathering and immediately all the carbon – black weapons, the Spraack, were raised toward Spar Tr and projection began at once. He absorbed the mass infusion of metabolic chrism, with his mane of white hair thrown back by the blast. His mantle of thick, luxuriant hair was his badge of office and honour. Only the Pe Spar Tr bore it, and it came from his first surviving of the mass projection of metabolisms. He'd been a warrior in his very youth. Then assistant to the politic Maks Fi and when Fi retired to Spon Sil Island, he became the politic, a post he had held for two hundred and thirty years with great flourish, skill and accomplishiment. When the reigning Spar Tr had finally died at nine hundred twenty seven, he had chosen the test and survived. After nine hours of metabol infusion he had the full mane. He was placed on the bane stone for a month of weeks, to recover and prepare to rule. He was wedded the following Spor Tr months to Usemi Aire. Their conjunction that year brought a seven-harvest Sun instead of the usual four and it was a good sign. His reign had been productive and generally trouble-free. At least until word had begun to trickle in to the planets from the egdes of the galaxies and beyond, of a being of four thousand years!! The first years of these stories saw the executions of those who dared to issue forth with what was obviously drivel and sacriligious treason. But then, one day during Caphorim Years, Scry Tharg himself had found their planets. He'd landed his monstrosity on Codal. 01-the Fel. For a month nothing happened. Then the gargantuan ship had opened its ugly tail, lowered a long, thin ramp and out roared the swordsman on his accursed two-wheel craft. Up and down the shiny Corian pavements of many villages and towns, severely wounding a Trick of security Warmen, who had tried to capture him. Then the abomination had laughed. He laughed! Especially at a relentless projection of metabols from the security Trick. He had absorbed enough technically, to White Mane and all he did was laugh! Then, this Earthling had had the sacriligious effrontery to try to make friendships. His crowning insult was to issue forth with what the Cyclids had heard for the first time in their existence, laughter. It crucified their subdued metabolism, their genetic reticence, their much sought-after and delicately acquired psyche. Worse than all that though, they had confirmed beyond doubt that he was older than four thousand years, as measured by their annular chronomets, which flanked every known entry corridor to their planets. Indeed, many of the delicate instruments were warped beyond repair trying to record an age they had never been programmed to accomodate. The abominate had roared off down the pave of one last village, boarded his immense craft and hit invultuate speed before any further Trickae could be deployed. The last the Endurion people had heard of him was his heinous laughter which seemed to spew forth from his craft even as it vanislied into pinlight.

Spar Tr spoke. "Krit Thelm up! "he commanded. Near the rear of the cavernous hall a Cyclid rose above the others, and then, forward to the Corian platform. Krit Thelm, a medical of reknown, former Gleamer Games Champion, decorated warrior, retired undefeated from the battle tables, stopped before the Spar Tr and then turned his back to the reignant. Below, the ten thousands gasped. "Thank you for your trust and courtesy Thelm. Up! "He commanded. Thelm turned and passed his weapon to a floating mandarin, a gesture of absolute servitude to the Master. Another gasp from thousands of sporil cavities. Cyclids never, ever unlimbed their weapons. That act rendered them perfectly harmless. "Again, thank you for your gesture Thelm. You are the one. He must die. Ash forever. Here is the vialus. Our scribe says it must go into his vascular system on an upper limb. One pressure is enough. The vialus contains enough to kill twenty like him if the Cyclids ever had such Cannetian unluck that such should ever be. "It was the longest speech Spar Tr had made in a hundred years. Thelm took the vialus from the Spar Tr. "You are gone Thelm. Witness and record his death. Failure makes you abominate. Do not! "He commanded and rose and vanished. Thelm floated out over the silent hall of Endurion. He looked down at the sea of disgust and hatred. He could feel hope there too, and, fear, for him. "He is not!" He shouted and raised the vialus. "I will watch and record!" Below the sea of sound washed over him like a blessing. "The abominate! The abominate!" Xe tzrect! Xe tzrect! "He floated away, far and away from the giant hall. He floated to a small hill, nearby, where he could see the lights and silhouettes of the village that was his home. He took the vial in his hands and studied it for a long time. It would utterly destroy Tharg in a matter of Earth days. 0h, yes. He could easily watch and record. Easily. He uncapped the vial and poured it out into the Endurion soil. It flared in bright light a moment and then it was gone. Had it been recorded that act would have been the most treasonous in Cyclid history. The darkest deed. The act most deserving of unsacred death. Hideous death. The Endurion people hated Tharg and wanted his vile, unholy existence to end the insult to the entire Endurion culture and histories. But Thelm hated Tharg more than that. He knew, had learned through other sacriligious means, that Tharg also wanted death. Prayed for it. Dreamt of it. Wanted it more than anything. and since it was a thing the swordsman wanted, since it was old Bladesgore's fondest wish, Thelm could not grant it. It would be a reward! The man must not have his wish. Instead he must suffer in the most hideous way possible for him. He must live and never, ever die! Thelm felt almost joy at the prospect of Tharg suffering, living in his own private hell for all of time, an abominate for ever even unto himself! Thelm turned his weapon upside down and pressed. A small opening appeared in the heel. He pressed again and a small, thin drawer slid out. In it was another vial. Inside the vial was a flame-red liquid which seemed to throb, to pulse. It seemed to be alive. Thelm held it to him and prayed the Disrepta, the Holy Disrepta. "Let me find him and kill him oh nSpar Trr. Kill him with life! Eternity!" And then he set out to find Tharg. And did.

CHAPTER NINE

A S KRIT THELM began his search for the Xe Trect, Tharg began his search for this year's Christmas family. For hundreds of years he'd returned to Earth at Yuletide searching for a special family to observe for the season. All the way back to the old planet he'd fill up Lapstrake's sound systems with ancient Terran Christmas music, all the old stuff, even Elvis Presley and Blue Christmas. His favourites were Gabriel's Message, the Coventry Carol, In the Bleak Midwinter, It came upon a midnight clear, Do you see what I see and a few others. Earth, of course, was no longer what it used to be. There were no industries left there of any kind, unless one considered the operation of retirement homes and certain tourist facilities as an industry. Earth had long ago given up its last renewable resource, a uranium deposit on the cold Labrador coast near Cartwright. The planet had been renewed ecologically to a great degree, even some species of fish came back and all the fresh water sources were renewed and purified of any contaminants. The population was only a couple of million now. Mostly seniors living out the remains of their lives in the quiet, tranquility of a planet that had once or twice destroyed itself in war. A few tourism agencies offered air travel tours around the contintential coastlines. You could still land in Lisbon and have a glass of wine in a small cafe outside the Belem Tower. You could still sit in the trenches of Beaumont Hamel and regret the youth of the world who had died there in July, 1916. You could still find a few nuns giving tours through the ruins of the Vatican. In Washington, the White House remained standing, restored many times over. You could let yourself in with an electronic EGO card and tour the old building by yourself if you were so inclined and weren't afraid of ghosts. Around the globe there were still some families who raised children the old fashioned way, with a Mom, dad and a few boys and girls or so. There was even a church or two around, in small communities in a few parts of Europe and North America, even in Iceland. There were still remnants of almost every race, colour, creed spread throughout the globe. Tharg had a record of each and every family on board Lapstrake, the ages of each member, occupation of the parents, address, attitudes on social issues, such as they were, religion if there was any, and Statement Of Existence which every Earthling had to make after age sixteen. This year he had found a small family in upstate New York, near where Lake Placid used to be. The father was a ski instructor with a small tourism outfit that had rights to the runs on Whiteface Mountain. The Belanger family, Merrill, his wife Anita, two sons, Charles and Philip and one daughter Lisa. Anita was a fully qualified teacher with a Masters Degree in Chemistry. Mr. Belanger had a degree in Philosophy with a Minor in Theologies. The boys, twins, were eleven and the girl, was seven. Mr. Belanger's Statement of Existence, his S. O. E. included his opinion that an Earth which could produce a poet who could write: "have you" the mountain, while his maples wept air to blood, asked "something a little child who's just as small as me can do or be? "god whispered him a snowflake llyes:you may sleep now, my mountain" and this mountain slept while his pines lifted their green lives and smiled was worth trying to save, and be near. He had also stated, to the great puzzlement of some, that . . ." As far as guitars go, the major chords tell the story and the minor chords tear out your heart. I love the minor chords.

Tharg's favourite poet was E. E. Cummings and he'd recognized the verse from (fire stop thief help murder save the world" in Cumming's still famous little tome 1x1. Tharg had done his thesis on Cummings for his Phd. in English Literature. Tharg knew every one of his poems off by memory. And he too loved the guitar, six and twelve string and he understood perfectly what Belanger had meant. Tharg wanted to see this fellow and his family. His wife's S. O. E. contained only two words: Earth is!

On December 23rd. Tharg put Lapstrake in orbit. He took a Quisar launch because it could hold a lot of small cargo and flew down to Mirror Lake, a few miles from the log cabin Merrill Belanger and his wife had built about twelve years ago. It was late at night. One of the pieces of equipment was a Novan Snow Jet that had a small invultuate engine, completely soundless. He got in and sped away towards the cabin. He could easily have studied every intimate detail of the Belangers on board Lapstrake using sophisticated observation equipment he employed sometimes tracking targets. He preferred at Christmas time, however, to do what he could, in person. He found the house on a small knoll in a little wood. He pulled in behind a few large pine trees and shut down his sled. He donned a Uni-ocular helmet with sound enhancement and scanned the area, finally focusing on the living room of the tiny lodge. A fire was burning in an old Vermont Casting's Stove. Small birch logs burned with a cheery attitude casting fireball reflections on the shiny Christmas Tree ornaments, giving the tree a life of its own, an involvement in the Christmas preparations. Mr. Belanger was hooking up a set of miniature lights on the tree. One boy, Philip was passing him things. The little girl Elisa was over in the corner arm chair winding up a tiny ceramic Christmas Tree that played Jingle Bells. The other boy, Charles was helping his mother in the kitchen making what looked like an old fashioned fruit cake. They were smiling and joking about this or that, observing, commenting, poking fun. A family. Tharg's eyes filled up. "Oh Lord, they're so beautiful. So happy. "Suddenly the little girl got up and went over to her daddy. "Don't forget papa. Tomorrow night we have to make a cake and leave it for Santa Claus. Her face held the brightest, reddest cheeks Tharg had ever seen, even in his old Christmas cards, which he had saved by the thousands, and still had, thanks to the age neutralizer an old soldier had given him once. "Booty I don't need Tharg. Take it! "Tharg had taken it and added it to the immense mountain of junk he had in Lapstrake on Deck Four, the Junkyard, "Oh, don't worry sunny brightspot. We won't forget Santa and we won't forget Baby Jesus will we little one?" The little girl suddenly became seriously reverent. "Oh no Papa. I'd never forget Baby Jesus. Can you sing the Friendly Beasts for us now?" The father smiled down at her, picked her up and hugged her. "You bet angel." Philip walked over to the big easy chair in the corner and reached behind to get the twelve string. He put it carefully in Mr. Belanger's hands. He tuned up a string or two and then sat down on a hard wooden stool by the piano and began to play the old tune. Then he began to sing and the children and his wife joined in . . . "Jesus our brother, kind and good, was humbly born in a stable rude, and the friendly beasts around Him stood, Jesus our Brother, kind and good." The song went on and on. Thargs eyes were soaked. He'd always like the last verse the best, "Thus every beast by some good spell, in the stable room was glad to tell, of the gift he gave Emmanuel, the gift he gave Emmanuel." When he finished Mr. Belanger said to his wife, "Hey hon, let's bake that cake for Old St. Nick right now and perhaps a little pudding for Baby Jesus too." They all shouted and cheered and went into the kitchen. Tharg put away his glasses and wiped his eyes. There was a full moon, lighting the night snow. The smell of the fire from the log cabin filled him with a nostalgic joy he always felt at this time of the year when he went to steal Christmas from some family. If he'd had a family of his own he'd build a little cabin like this for them too.

But a long, long time ago he'd stopped marrying and having families because it was just too hard saying goodbye time after time. Worse was watching little infants, childhoods, youths vanish before his eyes in the brief passage of their lives. Tomorrow night, Christmas Eve he'd come back once more, to see what he could see.

He got back into the sled and powered off. He sped through the night over the snow-covered landscape for hours, under old pine trees, down frozen river banks, by the relics of old farmsteads that had held stone farmhouses. He stopped by one great chimney still standing by itself in a field and took a photgraph of himself by the chimney with the Moon overhead. He was wearing a pair of old blue denim jeans, a red and black flannel shirt and an old soft leather Bomber jacket, of the kind worn by pilots in the early days of aviation His head was bare, but he had on thin leather gloves. Cold didn't affect him much except to make him miss the old days a little more. After a while he gathered some old pine branches and some kindling and built a little fire at the base of the chimney. The smoke rose in the windless night straight up the chimney and out to the Moon. The old spaceman stayed there until daylight took the Moon home. He went back to Lapstrake, but not before he'd carved his initials into the bark of a big old pine. ST-1999. He always used that date when doing something nostalgic on Earth. He ate and then, slept. He had to rest up for tonight, after all it was Christmas Eve!

The Belanger family had an old-fashioned sing-along until about 11:30 pm. They'd been drinking hot cider and chocolate all evening. Some presents were already placed under the tree and the watchful eye of the beautiful angel with her wand all lit up by miniature lights. Tharg watched from his distance in the grove of pines. He watched as the father finally opened the door and the little girl with the golden hair and red cheeks placed the tins containing the fruit cake for Santa and the pudding for Baby Jesus on the step. Just before her dad closed the door she looked up into the night sky, eyes on fire with wonder and curiosity. Then she kissed her palm and threw the kiss up, up, up into the sky to welcome the magic visitors who were to come. Tharg looked on, seeing the holy and magic event. Then the door closed and night tucked in the little family. The Family. Finally all the lights in the house were out and there was just a glow from the embers burning in the iron stove, Tharg crept over on the path to the house and took the two tins. In their place he put a Carettian Asca globe. It looked like a small ball of glass, but inside there were two tiny dancing creatures that resembled the beautiful Carettian Ascas themselves. It was an optical illusion thanks to a highly skilled artisan on Carett. Tharg knew the crystal couldn't be broken. The two crimson creatures never stopped their eternal dance as long as one held the little globe in the hand. The tiny gift was held inside a square little crate of pine Tharg had whittled last night. He'd engraved Merry Christmas Belangers in the wood. He leaned forward and kissed the front door of the log cabin and whispered the words himself.

Tharg never ever stayed after midnight, Christmas Eve. Lapstrake catapulted into skipjack almost as soon as he closed the landing bay doors. Below Mr. Belanger rolled over in his sleep, his mind telling him there was no such thing as thunder in the winter. Tharg sat in control, munching on homemade fruit cake, listening to The Friendly Beasts as sung by the Belanger family pouring out of his onboard speakers.

"Jesus my brother, kind and good . . .

CHAPTER TEN

THARG STARTED TO hear rumours about a plot the Endurions had to assassinate him while he was engaged in a coastal survey at the mouth of a galactic river in the Riga Astrabanks. He'd always known the Endurions hated him. They'd tried to do him in while he was there riding on Belinda once. He'd even tried to make friends with them. They had returned the offer of an outstretched hand with a blast of metabol. Had he been an ordinary human he would have been dead. That wasn't very polite and although it hadn't been funny either, he had laughed all the way out of the sector when he left because he knew the Cyclids psyche detested humour. He'd even heard it was against their religion. Lately, though, he'd been hearing rumours that made him think he might actually have to do something about the Endurion threat. He'd heard that their appointed assassin was Krit Thelm, a Cyclid he had encountered once before in a slave market auction. Tharg had taken a beautiful slave from Thelm, because the notion of enslavement always made him vicious. He'd been told a thousand times by supposedly civilized thinkers that he had no right to interfere in the cultural and social practices of other civilizations. He disagreed. "I guess I'll never be civilized," he'd always reply. He had destroyed the slave auction business and taken the slave with him. He'd laughed at Thelm all the while. The latest rumours about Thelm really worried and upset him. He'd heard that Thelm was abducting children from various outposts and remote planets whose security and police forces were no match for an Endurion-Obviously Thelm was well aware of Tharg's legendary love for children, all children and was trying to provoke him into a confrontation. Tharg was livid. He started leaving his own rumours around that he was coming back, looking for Thelm. He hoped that would stop the kidnapping, if they were true.

In the meantime he had been hearing more ugly stories about Blax and the accursed abomination Tharg thought he had put out of business, the Black Maria. It was now common knowledge that Blax was back in operation and his outrages growing more heinous by the minute. He was apparently now specializing in crippled or handicapped prisoners, although it was known he still had a penchant for children. On the good side of that bad news was a deep space communication Tharg had received from an official of Vulcan prison offering Tharg a way to put Blax out of commission permanently. Tharg was intending to do just that. Right now though, while in the Riga Astrabanks he thought he'd go see Emperor Vess of Riga, who had sent word he wanted to hire Tharg. The swordsman had heard a lot about the Rigans, the most interesting of which was that they had the Spalling larks(Kaltic Spallows in Rigan). Scry was not sure he believed in the Larks in the first place, but he'd like to find out one way or the other. The story was that the God who had created Riga had been attacked by four other Gods known as the Spalling. The reason for the attack was that Riga was located in a space considered the holy and exclusive demesne of the Spalling. Of course Gods don't bother to tell things like that to anybody else, including other Gods who might wander their way. So they hadn't even bothered to warn the Rigan God.

They'd just issued a divine decree that Riga God cease to exist. Well, that was a boo boo. Riga God had been in a very foul mood that day apparently, and he was a powerful and vindictive God. He brooked no interference, no insolence from anyone, especially other puny little Gods who thought to thwart him. There was a God battle then for the Spalling were very powerful as well and they were four, Riga one. After a while, no one knows how long for sure, it might have been minutes or centuries, Riga God had subdued the Spalling. Then there was the matter of suitable punishment, for as everyone knows, you cannot kill a God, much less four Gods. Finally Riga God turned the four into the Spalling Larks. He'd enclosed them into four tiny cocoons of his own divine energy and matter. Then to add insult to injury, after he had created Riga and the Astrabanks and populated it with a highly intelligent, capable and skilled race of people, the Vesscoluun, he gave the Larks to them to do with as they wished. They became to property of the first Emperor of Rigabanks to do with as he willed. They were of matchless value to whoever owned them because of what they could do for their owner. Anything. All one had to do was take the tiny cocoon in hand and smash it against any hard object. The God inside was released and would do any one thing for the owner before it was again free to be a free God. The cocoon couldn't be broken by accident. Volition was a necessary part of the release. One had to wish that the Spalling would be free to do one's bidding before it could be so. Throughout the history of the Riga Astrabanks no Emperor had ever used either of the Spalling. The Rigans were so capable, so good at taking care of their own problems that a suitable crisis or threat had never occurred. So they had been passed down from Emperor to Emperor.

Tharg was anxious to see if the fable was true. He brought Lapstrape down, down, down into the depths of the Rigan deep, for Riga was a planet submerged in oceans. The peoples lived and breathed under the seas of the waters that covered their world. Lapstrake, of course, was impervious to water, to pressure, to just about everything. As far as onboard systems went it did not matter if Lapstrake was whipping through deep space, burrowing through the mountains on some planet or resting idly at the bottom, in the waters of the deepest abyss. As his ship hooked up to a high transport tower, a great white tube linked his main portal to the tower's control and admission center. As he left his vessel he simply ordered Byter to "Secure!"

Emperor Vess thanked Tharg for coming and for the old gold coins he had given the young of Riga as he made his way to the Palace courts. Tharg often carried an old leather pouch full of gold coins of the kind minted in the 1300s in Spain. He'd give these to the young on various planets when he visited, unless he was in a hurry. Legend had it that a gold coin from Tharg would bring a child good luck and joy throughout life. The Rigans had humanoid forms without legs. Instead of legs they had a single trunk that ended in a fuzz-covered opening that was some kind of propellant. Some energy was emitted from that opening that sent the Rigans through the thin liquid of their world, at sometimes great speed. Otherwise they had two upper limbs, much like human arms except their's was a suction-like structure where the fingers would have been on one limb and a bony, grabbing configuration on the other. It reminded Tharg of the old fashioned toilet plungers. Their facial features were humanoid except their eyes bulged, there was no lid, and they had tiny fins where a human ear would have been. Tharg could detect no other opening in the Rigans and couldn't imagine how they fed or procreated. Emperor Vess was inside a long, wide upright tube filled with a thick green grease. He was swimming up and down the inside of the tube around a thin pole that was giving off sparks of black light. His voice was a warble.

"Rigan children will remember your generosity Scry Tharg. Forgive me this treatment but our physicians claim it keeps members of the Royal Family young and healthy. I'm not convinced, but the law is the law and we all must obey eh?" "As you say Your Highness."

"Mr. Tharg. You may call me Vess. Thank you for coming. I know this is your first time here and I hope you stay long enough to enjoy and satisfy your curiosities, although the matter I have called you for is urgent." "I am at your service Great Vess." "The Dach are stealing the water off our planet. They use it to make aquariums on their planet for their pets! We cannot attack because because they have my three children, held in one of their tanks. If we launch any kind of initiative they will drain the tanks at once. They came here on a mission of mercy, asking for a small quantity of our pristine waters. They claimed it was a medicine on their planet that could save thousands of lives. While their Ambassador was standing where you stand now, a squad of Dach soldiers entered the Royal Nursery above and took our children. And now they have them and we can do nothing. We cannot leave our planet without being incredibly obvious since our ships need vast tonnages of our lifegiving waters, and in any case, we are not very good at such offensives. We have always been able to defend what is ours from right here since all previous attempts to infringe on our existence have been direct assaults here. We can defend ourselves against any attack of that kind."

Silence.

"I know what you are thinking Mr. Tharg. You believe we have the Spalling Larks and therefore why don't we use one to solve this dilemma."

"Your High Vess, I would not presume to inventory Rigan treasures nor invade . . ." "Mr.Tharg, we have the Larks. The Spalling. But they cannot be used here. What most people do not know about them, and I have to take you into my confidence, and I worry not at all about it since your integrity is as famous as your skills with a blade, but the only qualifying restriction our people were given by God, our God, when the Larks were given to us was that they could not be used in any military operation. The restriction is on us and our honour, not on the Spalling. If I release one and command it to rescue my children, it can decide to accomplish this deed any way it wishes. I have no control over the outcome except I know my children will be returned. However, the Spalling could very well decide to kill everybody on Dach! You, Mr. Tharg, are our only hope, and our need is urgent because they are taking our waters at a formidable pace. Please help."

"Your Highness. I might have to kill a few Dach myself in order to carry out this mission."

"Although the loss of any life is as unpleasant to us as it is to you Sir, we believe we have the right to defend what is ours and in the past we have had to take life from others. We regret and mourn these actions still. But, sometimes it is necessary. We cannot allow the Spalling to do this, but we, ourselves, must and there is no constraint on us except for our own moralities and very real grief. I do not ask you to do this thing lightly."

Tharg bowed to the Emperor Vess. "I will go back to my ship and study this problem. Then I shall decide."

"Again Master Tharg, thank you for coming, for the coins and my offer to you of Rigan hospitality is open to you regardless of your decision."

Tharg studied the problem for three days. With Byter he studied every bit of information he had of the two cultures, the Dach, the Riga. Finally he decided to go to Dach and try and reason with them to give up the children on their own. He'd offer them a substitute for Rigan liquids, using his own laboratory, so that they. would not need to take from the Rigans again.

As he was preparing to leave for Dach, Byter spoke. "An incoming vessel, fully armed, approximately three hours away. Commanded by Master Blax. He's been ordered to Dach to pick up three Rigan children."

CHAPTER ELEVEN

THE BLACK MARIA barged its way through another meteorite field. The prison ship was of such massive bulk that it could bump off meterorites the size of small asteroids. Blax wasn't concerned. Tharg was near. He could smell him. He had not waited to find out what the Harllan was going to do for him. He had been ordered to Dach to pick up three children, a treat in itself, but even more so when he found out they were Rigan. He had never had any prisoners from the waterworld before. It was promising to be a truly delightful trip and then, his onboard systems had detected a vast spaceship, not Rigan, lying in the waters there. On further scansion he discovered the ship was the despicable Lapstrake. Even the name made him rage. Now he had to figure out how to capture the ship and its only crew member. From what he'd heard of the weapons systems on board, her intelligence capabilities, her speed and shields security, he believed he could quit forever this prisoner trafficking and go out on his own, on Lapstrake and then take whomever, he wanted, whenever, wherever and however he wanted. "Whyever was obvious." He smiled to himself.

Tharg had warned the Rigans of the approach and the mission of the Black Maria. The Rigans had set their weapons systems on load and aimed in the direction Blax was coming. Then he took Lapstrake off the planet and into a high orbit over the shipping lane. He waited. He got out his sloppy little black binder, all patched up with old beige packing tape. On the cover marked on a piece of tape was DARK THINGS, hand-printed in thick black ink. Inside, the yellowed pages were full of scribbled notes and memos about things he needed to know or remember. They concerned inexplicable or disgusting or really evil phenomena, or places, or creatures. He knew he had an entry in there about Blax, some important piece of data about the prison master monster. "Aha! Here it is!" Blax hates certain kinds of poisonous snakes. Hates them and has an horrific, irrational fear of pseudechis. Apparently it was an infestation of snakes that had wiped out half the population of his home planet before the authorities had found a way to get rid of them. Blax had lost his entire family and had been covered by dozens of them, but somehow managed to survive, even though he had been bitten many times. Bitten and chewed. "Hmmmm. pseudechis, "Tharg thought. A plan was forming. The Master of Lapstrake chuckled. Blax would not have enjoyed that sound any more than the Endurions. Nope.

A little later Blax was straining to contain his excitement. He was getting closer and now he knew how he would capture the slave-lover, the Earthling with the stupid swords. He knew now. Tharg would surrender! Blax had done a little homework. He had found out all about Riga, all about Dach, all about the children Dach had requested be picked up and now he knew why Tharg was here. The Children's God some called him. Childlover. Tharg the sook. Tharg was here to rescue the children! It was obvious.

They were Rigan. Clearly, abducted in some political or military strategy by the Dach. Blax also knew the Rigans hardly ever left their planet, that they were incompetent off-world. Tharg was supposed to be their hero. Once again. But Blax would get the children first and then offer to set them free in exchange for Tharg's surrender in a prison-tube. Tharg would have to agree or risk, not only losing the children, but disgracing his name forever by failing to deliver for the first time, on a contracted deal. Tharg's famous handshake. "Baby's Blood!" His onboard intelligence equipment, his Book of Knowledge, he called it, was suddenly warning him of the fast approach of a small craft. No one at the controls. No human life on board. Blax suspected right away it might be the Dach pilot launch sent out to guide him in. It must be on auto-guide. He flicked on his optic-vids and had a look. It was Dach all right. His armaments were on the ready and coded to fire if the launch made even an aggressive wink. He ordered the Book of Knowledge to lock on to the vessel and tractor it into one of the landing shelves. Then he went down to have a look inside.

Meanwhile, Lapstrake was orbiting in close proximity to Dach and Scry was asking permission to land. He wasn't getting a response. He put another call into Byter and sent again. Nothing. Okay. Fine. He opened up a telecommunication mike with a broadcast satellite hookup and cleared his throat. "Ahem! People of Dach. Tharg here. You know me. I am a man of honour. I want no trouble and mean you no harm. I have an interesting piece of equipment on board my ship. Back on my planet Earth, a long time ago this equipment was used to remove salt from sea-water so that mariners would not need to carry so much water with them and waste valuable cargo space, especially on long trips. Smaller versions of this equipment also came in handy if your ship went down and you ended up lost at sea with no provisions. I have done a little modification to this equipment using Rigan water to experiment with and guess what? My little machine can now produce Rigan water from the elements that make up Dachan atmosphere. Isn't that interesting! With a little ingenuity and hard work, bigger models of this machinery could be built with formidable capabilities. Now, my question is this . . . do you want it? Tharg out.

It was an hour before they answered and just before they responded Tharg thought he heard screaming, insane screaming, on several incoming transmissions. It sounded a lot like Blax. The old duellist smiled. He smiled a lot. Pseudechis. "Hee. Hee."

Then Lapstrake was hit by a vicious frick-pulse from the Dach weapons batteries in a mountain range north of the capital, Aclia-dacli, in the Eastern grid of the Kingdom. "Interesting answer, "he said into old VOX microphone. "Tsk. tsk. I guess this means that you are not all that interested in my little salt shaker. In that case the Rigans can have it." He hit skipjack and went back into high orbit, out of range of the Dach cannon below. Now he needed a new plan. "I guess it'll have to be a little more "hands-on".

A hundred thousand kilometres away, on board the Black Maria which was still hurtling through space toward Dach, the badly bitten body of Blax lay on the landing shelf, alongside the Dach pilot ship replica Tharg had hastily put together on Lapstrake. There was no pseudechis of course, there never were. But the small launch had been blocked-full of Rigan water and the water had been heartily stocked with Emperor Vess's pet eels, which he kept in sealed vinegar tanks, their natural environment, at the Palace. They were harmless to Rigans but their hollow, needle-like teeth were full of venemic, a poison to all others, that was fatal, within hours. One bite from a Rigan eel and you die horribly, slowly. When Blax hit the seal lock to open the doors to the launch, tons of Rigan water crashed into him, knocking him to the floor of the landing shelf. The water contained about five hundred frightened, vinegar-starved Rigan eels. Blax had screamed into the open communication spokes on the collar of his nav-vest. It was linked into Black Maria's main communication transmits. As the venemic poison hit his central nervous system, it paralyzed him completely, without shutting off his sensory plant. The agonies that for him, were just beginning, did nothing to block his cognitive abilities to reason what had happened. His rage was all the more egregious in his impotence, his inability to act and the very knowledge of that fact. He couldn't even voice the torrent of black invective being formed in what was left of his mind. Complete insanity was denied him, however, as his Herculean will tried extravagantly to circumvent the chemical and invisible bonds that held him motionless. He couldn't even snarl. The mindless pain was unable to gain him any lenience from the venemic prison in which his blood was drowning. He died after a while, never having given sound to the screaming of his crucified body and soul, tiny Rigan eels swimming in and out of every opening in his flesh. He died knowing Tharg had beaten him again, taking away, forever, his greatest treasure, his ability to pleasure himself by inflicting pain on others. He died unable to curse the Earthling, silently praying nevertheless, to the Gods of the darkness, to rid the Universe of the accursed, interfering Childsaver.

Tharg sent another transmission over the old VOX. "People of Dach. For your own information I wish to report that the colossally despicable prison ship known as the Black Maria, is headed straight for your planet, completely out of control, at invultuate speed. There is no one at the Thelm, er, ah, I mean helm. The unfortunate Blax has met with a totally sad accident and as old Darth Vader never said . . . . He won't be back! So, I advise you to act accordingly. If I could help you, which, actually, I could, I would, but, let's face it, I don't want another blast from one of your detonate cannon, now do I? Tharg out. Ciao!"

On another channel Tharg received a message from Emperor Vess. It said, don't know what's going on up there. Stop. Glad Blax is out. Stop. And can't get his oily hands on my children. Stop. Are we now back at square one? Stop. Scry sent him a quick TX to stand-by, for the outcome of a deadly game of poker, and "Trust me." Out.

No word from the Dach.

He opened up his microphone again. "I guess you people are aware of the staggering store of munitions old Blax has collected and stored over the years on board that ship. As you know he was completely insane and one aspect of that insanity was total paranoia. He thought everybody wanted to attack him. God only knows why he thought that." Tharg closed the mike and tried to stop from laughing. "In any case that ship is loaded for bear as they used to say when there used to be bear. Well, I guess I'll be heading out of here now so good luck you people down there on Dach. I just hope the folklore about Blax having a pou sto bomb on board was just another fairy tale. You know those things get their name from the old Greek saying . . . Where I may stand. That's because once it hits its target it detonates. Then it detonates. Then it detonates again. And keeps on detonating from the same location, in ever-widening circles of destruction until its last pulse of destruction fails to encounter any other matter of any kind, in other words when there isn't anything else left to detonate.

When that happens it regresses to an old-fashioned nuclear and simply destroys itself and any other planets in the vicinity. Nah! That can't be true. Not even Blax hated people enough to carry something like that around. Did he? Out!"

Tharg ordered Byter to prepare for launch. Byter told him they were being probed by Dach. The Dach now knew he was preparing to skipjack. "Give us an old-time countdown Old Stocking, "He told Byter. "Ten!" "Nine!" "Eight!" "Seven!" "Six!" "Five!" "Four!" "Three!" "Two!" "One!"

"Tharg!!!"

"Hold Byter".

Tharg looked behind him and stared into the tinted visor of a Dach General.

"I heard the Dach had perfected molecular transmission, but had always believed the gene issue had rendered that theory obsolete. Guess I was wrong. Welcome. Lapstrake and I welcome you aboard General. I'd sure like to learn how to do that sometime."

"Does Blax have a pou sto on board?"

So much for pleasantries.

"Can't be certain. You know they are easily disguised. There's only one sure way of knowing and that is when it goes off. Then you know he did."

"I should kill you for interfering. You know he was on official Dach business coming here."

"Anything's possible."

"We know you can easily stop his ship Straker, or alter its course. Do it now! Hurry!"

"Straker. Hmmm. I wondered what the Dach called me-Hurry! Hurry! Listen did I ever tell you the story of the old bull and the young bull? See those two were down in a meadow, grazing. Up on the nearby hill were a dozen or so female bulls and they were looking pretty foxy. So the young bull says to the old bull that they should run up that hill and make love to one of them sweet things. But the old bull, well he called that young feller aside and said "Son, let's take our time and walk up that hill and make love to them all. "So, do you see my point General? Sometimes people are in too much of a hurry for their own good."

"Okay Tharg. What do you want?"

"Hmmm. Well, before we can even begin negotiations I want those three children sent back to Riga and I want it done in the next sixty seconds."

"No. It can't be done. That's official Dach business. You have no right to interfere."

"Byter start again."

"Ten!" "Nine!" "Eight!" "Seven!" "Six!" "Five!"

"Stop! Okay Earthling! The children have been sent home." Byter's circuits flared and whirled and then Byter confirmed that the children were on their way back to Riga. Tharg got up and started stretching his long legs by leaning against a bulkhead. "Okay now we're getting somewhere. I have only two other minor conditions. The first is an Official Royal Decree from the Dach Monarch that the Dach will never again contact, in any way, the Rigans or go near their world. Second, I want you to show me how you got here."

The Dach officer didn't move but Tharg could hear soft, electric garbling coming from inside the visor. "It is done. The Rigans have the decree and your copy is in that thing you called Byter. As for the other request, shake my hand.

Tharg shook his hand.

CHAPTER TWELVE

THE TINY FIRE burned with a golden brightness. The smell of smoking birch and pine, intoxicating. A lone figure sat by the brave blaze warming his hands against the flame, a billion bright stars above, dreaming all he could, with all his might. Scott Robert Thorne, Earthling, alias Scry Tharg. He often sat out on his hull, lit an oxygen-enhanced camp-fire, pitched a tent and slept out under the stars. It depended on the night. If he was travelling through a sector where the stars were special. Sometimes he would play his guitar and sing fireside songs. He even wrote a song about it once. "I sit by the fire, sing fireside songs or out on the sea, sing sea-shanty songs . . ." Often he would play for hours. Lapstrake could project an alcove of Earth atmosphere around where he was siting. It supplied oxygen for the fire and air for him to breathe. He used the hull a lot. He jogged on it. Performed all his martial arts kata and weapons training there.

As he sat by the fire he thought of all the things he had learned just before he left Riga and Emperor Vess. For one thing, he now could do that neat little trick General Proulx had used to get aboard

Lapstrake. The Dach had found a simple way of maintaining genetic integrity by transfering all of the molecules without interfering with the genetic structure. At the last minute, on a whim, Tharg had given the Dach general the little device he had re-wired to produce Rigan water. He'd figured that there would then be even less motivation for the Dach to ever consider bothering the Rigans again. The complement of prisoners on board the Black Maria had contained enough qualified persons to run the ship. Tharg turned it over to them and recommended they head for any of the abandoned planets in uninhabited space. Before they left he had supervised the destruction of all the hideous reminders of Blax. His weapons of torture, his store of photographic horrors, his illegal weapons, his prisoner holding cells, the Playroom. The entire ship was scrubbed down with ionic gravel, re-done in bright colours, inside and out. All records of all prisoners erased. Anything that could ever be used by anyone to coerce anyone else had been destroyed. There had been no pou sto bomb on board, of course, as Tharg had known. The Rigans and Lapstrake had replenished any low stores on board and in an official ceremony the Emperor Vess had granted official amnesty to all prisoners on behalf of the Royal Kingdom of Riga. That made them all feel good as they set out on their new adventure and a new life. Those who claimed innocence and whose claim could be verified by deep space communication, were sent back to their homes on board Dach freighters. Some of these, after having proven their innocence, stayed on the Black Maria and took the offer of a new start anyway. The vessel was renamed Splanethrake. Tharg stood on the upper hull canopy of his own ship and saluted the new pioneers as they slowly moved out of orbit and sailed away. He could see the newly-sealed hole his own guns had burned into the ship when he vaporised the landing shelf that had held the rictus of horror that once had been Blax. Lapstrake set off a broadside of cannon fire as the Rigans sent up nitrogen fireworks and the saved passed by. A baby born to a young girl who still had one arm left, was christened Scott Robert as they pulled away. Emperor Vess had given Scry Tharg a Kaltic Spallow, as the older Rigans called them. In an elaborate ceremony that thoroughly embarrassed the scarred swordfighter the Emperor's smallest child, Warn, had presented the Lonesome Human with the greatest treasure of the known worlds, in the histories of the knowns. Tharg had been seated facing the Rigan throne. The child had come to him, pried open his fist and laid the sacred object in his palm, then closed the fist, bowed, kissed the fist, and backed away. The throne room was full of dignitaries and special guests from across the nearby Gulags Immuninati and beyond. All three of the rescued children kissed Thargspore. The Emperor's mate had been dead for many years but all the Rigan women in attendance bowed to the Spallowlord. They bowed.

The Spalling Lark felt warm, alive in his palm. Tharg's right eye throbbed, pulsed, and turned a soft violet-blue as it always did these days, when he was in the vicinity of magic or supernatural power. He opened his fist. It was as if a small firestorm raged out of control, yet contained by his hand. It did not burn. The tiny object seemed to be a thousand tiny clouds of flame or so many shades of red and orange and other colours held never seen before, all swirling, moving, spinning around inside an oval-defined configuration, an egg of Divine power. Tharg felt healed. Powerful beyond all telling. He felt right and proper, as if he had found his place and his fist was telling. There was no containment whatsoever. The Spallow was not enclosed in any kind of matter that Tharg could see or feel. It did not burn him, but he had never felt so moved in his long life. He was overwhelmed by such a yearning, an inhumanly vast gasping for, for . . . freedom. Tears poured from his eyes and floated onto the Kaltic Spallow. That yearning consumed him. It was neither corrosive nor coercive. It was simply that he felt the truth of the God in his palm, His need! The Rigans sat in awe as Tharg stared down at the most exquisitely pretty sight his eyes had ever beheld. In the thin liquid of the Rigan water his salty tears seemed golden as they floated down and away. His tears were heavier than the Rigan life-water and therefore dropped through it, like gold. He closed his fist gently. He looked at Emperor Vess. "I may do with the Spallow as I wish?"

"As you wish Honoured Tharg. It is a God. It's duty is to you. It can do anything but war for you. Bring you anything you desire. Make you old enough to die. Young enough to be back on Earth four thousand years ago before you became what you are. Anything. It is yours. whatsoever you will, you may do. It is the wish of the Rigan people that what you wish you will have, for you have given us back our lives and our future. We can never repay you for this.

Tharg opened his fist. He stared at the God in the tiny clouds of storm.

FREEDOM! FREEDOM! FREEDOM!

He smashed it against his chair and shouted, I want you to be free. That is my desire for you. Be!!!"

Emperor Vess fell to the side and was caught by a court Guard. Many women swooned. Several high-ranking officers of the guard pointed their weapons at Tharg. The most universally expressed sentiment in the hall was, "NO!" "NO!" "Sacrilege! "was also heard in some quarters. The Spallow was still rising upwards in the watery medium of the Rigan world as the citizens of that planet gasped and stared at Scry Tharg in shock and horror. Then that world detonated with power. The oval of divinity exploded. All those colours, those fires and flames of power, clouds and storms of omnipotence filled up the whole world of Riga in an instant and a voice that could be heard across the galaxy roared two words "FREEDOM THARG!" and vanished.

In the sudden silence that was instantaneous afterwords Tharg felt exquisite relief. He felt it in his soul and he no longer felt alone there either.

He approached the throne. "Scry Tharg thanks you for the matchless honour of having visited your court and your people. He thanks you for sharing your world with him. Your perfect hospitality. He thanks you most of all for the most precious gift he has ever been given, a chance to free a God. I have never felt so honoured and will never again as I do this day. My name is Tharg-No one is my slave-No one does my bidding-I serve whom I chose to serve. I wish this for all peoples, everywhere. Even the Gods, for I serve no God either. My creed; FREEDOM!"

He saluted, bowed and backed away towards the entrance. No one spoke as he left. They never saw him again.

The fire on his hull was burning out. He put on a small junk of maple. He had a great supply of wood from home onboard. He liked to whittle sometimes. He made his own bow and arrows, usually of yew. He made his own walking staffs and carved intricate runes in them in many languages. Tonight he was carving an old saying he believed his mother used to sing to him when he was a boy.

"Little man you're crying, I know why you're blue. Someone stole your kiddy car away. Little man you've had a busy day."

That was all he could remember. A long time ago when he had come to realize he wasn't going to age and perhaps not die for a while, he had set about writing down and recording many things that he could remember about his life so that he could be accurate in recall, years later. He'd kept up his records, and still had a great many volumes stored in his library on discs of every kind, but also many in their original, written form in paper journals. His age neutralizer kept them in decent shape.

He leaned back and rested his head on his arms, looking out at the stars. He thought about the Kaltic Spallow. He felt a great peace come over him. He seemed at peace with the Universe this night. He started to hum an old Brenda Lee tune, "Is it true the talk that's gonna round the town . . ."

After a few bars, he fell asleep. Up above, the stars shined and twinkled and winked. Up above them, a billion more stars did the same thing. Way up above all the stars and beyond the edge of nothingness, way, way beyond, a God with eyes like a storm of fires looked down, down, down. Down at the sleeping figure of the lonely man. The lonely man who wasn't sure if he wanted to live or die. The lonely man who needed something more than anything else. The lonely man who needed love, a love pure and true and only.

Love that only a God could grant.

A God who would have to love the lonely man very much to bring him such a gift.

The gift of love.

CHAPTER THIRTEEN

THARG MET CON Hall when he bumped into Lapstrake with his head. The ship's sensory equipment was so sensitive that it had known there was something floating around outside the hull for a few hours. He flicked on screen and watched as an apparently unconscious, huge, human just sort of hung there in the void, hardly moving at all. Scry had a well-proven policy of watching and observing things that appeared near his craft before ever doing anything to approach it. The man was wearing a very old space suit, looked like an old PFD Series, probably 888, a body fitting cover of sealed gases necessary for whatever life form was wearing it and toughened to withstand space debris somewhat. Tharg's equipment could detect nothing on the body, no weapons, there was life, he was still breathing, and a small flask of some kind of liquid. Finally he hauled the man on board and brought him to Medic Six on a trolley. He removed the space coveralls and hooked the man up to Byter's diagnostic banks. He found nothing wrong with the man, except he was overweight, had bad lungs, was in poor phsyical condition, and was apparently, very drunk.

"That's disgusting Byter. I thought humans had given up that dirty old habit a thousand years ago. "Byter sounded solemn whenever he decided to do a little pontification. God! That men should put an enema in their mouths to steal away their brains;that we should, with joy, pleasance, revel, and applause, transform ourselves into beasts."

"That's enemy you metal ning-nong. Enemy. That God should put an enemy in their mouths to steal away their brains . . ." Don't you know the difference between an enema and a glass of two hundred year old scotch? Ya nimrod nuncbinc! "The fat man had suddenly sat up and was trying to disengage himself from Byter's electrodes. Byter was silent. "Don't worry sir, he'd never make that mistake again. Byter never makes the same mistake twice. My name is Tharg sir, Scry Tharg. And you? "Tharg extended his left hand. He always shook hands with his left so that his sword hand was free. Even though he was as good with his left as he was with his right in any swordplay. You never know. "Well obviously he wasn't built by humans, if he never makes the same mistake twice." "Actually he was made on Qua by . . ." Good Lord! I know what they have on Qua. I was right. He wasn't made by humans, but by what once were humans, if indeed, there are more than one and the jury's still out on that n'est-ce pas? En tout cas je m'appelle Con Hall. Enchante de faire votre connaissance. Moi j'ai soif! "With that he reached over to the table of medical instruments by his side and took the flask Tharg had taken from him. He pulled a grubby little cork from the top and took a long, long draught. "Ahhh. There is a God. Hell there are many Gods! Yes sir Mr. Tharg, many Gods. By the way son where are we and how did I get here?" Then he took another swallow. Tharg smiled. "Well sir, if you don't know how you got here I can't help you. Byter couldn't find any tangible evidence on your space suit to identify your last landing on solid ground. It's as if you had been washed off somewhere, cleansed of any evidence that might identify you. In any case, you are on board my ship, Lapstrake, and we are headed to Deneb in the Cygnus constellation. I can drop you off anywhere you would like in the other direction, after I finish my mission.

That would be fine Mr. Tharg. I don't remember how I got here for some reason. The last thing I can remember is that I was having a sip at a pub called the Three Maggies, not exactly sure what planet that was. I used to be a costermonger a long time ago, but gave it up for the life of a space mariner. I been swabbing the deck for sixty years now sir, in a manner of speaking. I got no family, my home is the stars when I can get a berth on board some scow or other. I do like a wee drop o' the Creature, especially good scotch and every now and then I like to get my beard trimmed by a pretty lady. So, when do you think we might be heading back, a week or so?" "Approximately four years!" "Are ya bleeding mad! I'll be too old to work by then man. Can't ya drop me off somewhe . . ." Lapstrake was rocked by a terrific jolt, as if she'd hit an iceberg head on, at full speed. Byter "One hit from a Cack Pulse on the control canopy. An extremely dangerous way to open a conversation. It's a Spark Warship from Wislings Spinq the Nations. They sent a message as they fired that warning shot. They want the ignorant man."

"Hee hee. I'll have to go to the library later and check out Shakespeare myself to see which one of you is right. Although there's something that doesn't smell right about enema. Ha. Ha. Engage the Ion Bucklers and arm full up! I need to talk to those people and tell them how very rude they are."

Con Hall rubbed his grey whiskers and got down from the trolley. "Seems to me that crowd needs a good caning. They got the manners of a louse! Get me a pistol Mr. Tharg and I'll help ya blast them into civility. It's the only way with some people. Oh my God! Did you say Scry Tharg. You're Scry Tharg! You're Scry Tharg! My God! Bladesgore! Knifesinger! Please Mr. Tharg I didn't mean to bump into your ship. I don't even know how I got here or why that crowd is after me and I certainly don't want no duel with you sir. Hail Mary, full of Grace, the Lord is with thee "The man made the sign of a cross over his bloodshot eyes, and paled visibly as Tharg hit a rank of switches and buttons, and passed his hands over a long thin panel holding multi-coloured triangles and squares and other shapes.

He pulled the VOX Mike towards him, ignoring the Earthman who was now on his knees, alternately praying and taking a swig from his flask. "This is Scry Tharg, Commander of Lapstrake, the ship you Sparks just dented pretty badly and for which you shall pay. Please do not fire again. Tell me why you want the Earthman and tell me why you didn't ask before you fired. Your answer may be a very important determinant as far as you people making retirement age goes. Tharg out."

Byter, "They are reloading the Cack.

"Is that old SCUD Missile still on board?"

"Yes Captain. It hasn't been tested though for a long time."

"If they fire again, launch the SCUD. Those things have been obsolete for so many years the Sparks will think I have discovered a new weapon."

"There's a message coming in now Captain."

"Let's hear it Byter.

"Commander Tharg. The people of Wislings Spinq the Nations do not explain themselves to anybody, especially a well known criminal like you. You were slapped on the wrist for having the audacity to remove our property in the first place. That man committed serious crimes in our jurisdiction, the most major of which was he drank the Sacred and Holy Sanguia. We could have killed him, but in our great and famous compassion sentenced him to fifty years exile in space, instead. If you look at his neck you will see his crimes listed there. We want him back now. You have fifteen seconds to answer."

Tharg grabbed Hall by the scruff of the neck. Sure enough, tatooed into his neck, behind his head were a series of markings, that he didn't recognize. They were marked into a tiny square of shaved skin. Tharg dragged the drunk to his feet. "What the hell is Sanguia. Answer quickly we have ten seconds left." "I think I'm going to be sick. "He started to turn. Tharg picked him up off the floor with his left hand until the man was two feet off the deck. "Sanguia."

"It's the blasted wine they use in some of their religious ceremonies, weddings, funerals, ordinations, executions. I couldn't help it. I bought it off some sod before I knew what it was and when I tasted it I couldn't help myself. Lord it was the sweetest, smoothest drink I've ever had in my life! God what I wouldn't give for a glass now. It makes you feel ten feel tall too and there's no gueule de bois. Imagine no sickness at all the next day! I didn't know what it was. The guy who sold it to me should be hove off in space not me. I told them all that in court!"

"You and I have to have a long talk about your lifestyle choices Mr. Hall. Byter open up VOX. He pulled the microphone over to his mouth. "'Attention the Spark ship. This is Captain Scry Tharg of the spacehip Lapstrake. His ship suddenly rocked and rolled over as if she had been caught in a hurricane off the Horn. "That was a direct hit to our southern wing peripheral. SCUD has been launched and has blown out the Cack Gun battery. The Spark ship has moved away, out of range of the SCUD."

Tharg cursed "Pilate's fist! "he slammed his fist into his palm." It's just as well for ya to hand me over to them Mr. Tharg. They'll give me another flask and fling me out the door again. What odds."

"You know what Mr. Hall. That's a very good idea. Byter tell the Sparks they can have Mr. Hall. An hour later Hall was taken on board a Spark shuttle and brought back on board their ship.

"Captain Tharg. I shall have to agree to disagree as to who was in the wrong today, but since you have returned our property we will not retaliate for your insubordination. However, do not enter Spark territory again without an invitation." The transmission ended and Tharg told Byter to begin repairs to the ship. Then he went to the galley for tea and tomato soup cake, his favourite sweet. And waited.

Early the next morning Byter reported that someone was knocking on a porthole on the starboard wings. "I think it's the man who misquotes Shakespeare sir and who smells like a two-hole outhouse." Tharg laughed Where the catspit did you hear that one Byte? ""You said it approximately seventeen thousand hours, fourteen minutes and eight seconds ago during that incident with the derelict zoo station. "Let him in Byter and clean him up before he comes to me."

"I did as you told me to Mr. Tharg. As soon as I got taken on Board their ship, they put me in irons and threw me in the brig. Then I started singing a few old sea shanties. They told me to shut up. I told them Sanguia made me want to sing. They went nuts. They entered my cell, grabbed the flask, opened it and took a sniff. Game over. Watever you put in there, became a gas as soon as they opened it. These little nose plugs you gave me did the trick. I was not affected at all. In about four minutes everyone on board was out stone cold. As if they'd been lid down on the daybed all day with a forty."

"Did you put the virus into their memory racks and verify as I showed you?"

"Yes sir. It will show, when they wake up that their mission was a success. I was recaptured, but died on the way back to court. There is no record of any encounter with you Mr. Tharg, they won't remember a thing, and guess what?"

"What's that Mr. Hall? "Hall pulled out a huge leather sack of some kind and started squirting liquid from it down his throat. "Sanguia!"

"You know Mr. Hall. I think it's going to be a long four years with you aboard, but probably not very dull."

Hall laughed. He said, "You know Captain, if I had a degree in ethology like you probably have, I'd probably be able to figure me out, but since I don't, what odds. Have a squirt?"

"No thank you Mr. Hall."

"Well in that case ya haven't got a smoke on ya have ya?"

CHAPTER FOURTEEN

"KEEP YOUR HULL clean Thorne. You never know when it will mean the difference between Death and Life. "The words haunted the swordsman. Came into his mind unbidden, often just before he fell asleep. There was something about them that bothered him. Something not right. Some hook there somewhere. That creature in the Bootes Helix field who'd claimed he was God. "Pook!" He'd met some weird people. Poor old Con. Now there was a weird one. He missed him. It had been just as painful as all the other times saying goodbye to loved ones. Hall had stayed on board Lapstrake for seven years. He was the only crewman Tharg had ever hired. Actually he hadn't actually hired him, just eventually started to pay him because once he, was aboard and realized he was on for a while he started working. Tharg discovered the old sop could do many things. He'd picked up many skills. He had even managed to catalogue The Junkyard, Tharg's massive accumulation of odds and ends from all his years in space. Hall had built special holding shelves, racks and tanks and spaces and now the place was neat as a pin. One of the collections of things he'd found as he picked his way through all that memorabilia was a staggering supply of vintage wines and spirits. Tharg had found him crying in his stateroom one day and was told by the old man that he was just so happy, he couldn't help it. Later, Byter, when updating Tharg on Hall's progress he'd told him of the find. Tharg knew then that Hall was crying because of his great dilemma. He would not steal from the Swordsman as a matter of honour and he would never ask for anything because he was already so grateful to him.

"Would you do me a big favour Con?"

"Try and think of something I wouldn't do for you Captain just try."

"Would you mind getting rid of some of those old bottles of alcohol down the the Yard. I'm afraid some of them might be explosive, after fermenting for so long. Just destroy them any way you like. Don't touch any of the stuff from Earth, if they look stable to you, but all the rest, well, take care of it for me would you?"

Con started to choke. A combination of emotion and too big a bite of Byter's ration cake.

"I'll do me best sir. Sniff."

Con had died saving Tharg and Lapstrake from destruction. The Sparks had eventually figured out the trick Tharg had played on them and finally tracked them down near a covey of small planets just off the Helprin Solar system. Byter confirmed that they had a pou sto rocket on board. Tharg's buckler shields would be no good against the pou because, although it could not penetrate the bucklers, it didn't need to. It would attach itself to the shield and start detonating. It wouldn't take long for the bucklers to break down and then Lapstrake and the tiny planets and possibly the Helprin Sun would be gone. Tharg knew that if the Sun went, it would have unimaginable consequences for the stability of the entire galaxy, and possibly nearby solar systems. It could set off a catastrophic concatenation of events that would reach as far as all of the known worlds. His only hope would have been if he could somehow trick the Sparks into firing the rocket into a nearby Black

Hole. Tharg knew the Hole could absorb the pou make it just another part of the dense matter of the Hole before it could harm anything. But he couldn't think of a plan that could get them to do that. He knew they'd fire at him as soon as they got into range and not risk a deceit like the last time. Tharg decided to surrender. He had ordered Byter to shut down all his weapons systems even before the Sparks had come into range. The last time he'd seen Con he'd been draining another relic from the Wine Cellar, as he now called the Junkyard. So, Tharg was shocked when Byter told him Hall had launched a Lancer Bike and that he had taken the remains of Dr. Brougham, the old geneticist who had made Scott Robert Thorne immortal. Tharg cursed and swore. "Catspit and Pilate's Fist. What's that old fool up to. He must be inebriated." "Actually Captain Tharg he is inebriated. I believe he has taken the remains of the Scientist so that the Sparks will believe that you have accompanied him on the Lancer. When they probe the vessel two humans will be the reading. They will conclude you and Hall are making an escape attempt. By the way Captain, he is heading straight for the Helprin Black Hole. I don't think he can be stopped now. The Lancer has skipjack thrust.

"Byter bring us around before the Sparks fire." "Too late Captain! They've launched the pou sto. It's heading straight for the Lancer!"

"Oh Con! Con! Old son. Old sod. Old devil!"

The pou sto hit the Lancer and detonated as it entered the Hole. There was one savage wave of destructive energy from it that rocked Lapstrake violently, and then the Universe returned to normal. The bomb had become debris in the infinite density of that hole in the void. "Power up the ululate battery and fire at the Spark. Disable!"

Byter fired before Tharg was finished. The blast tore off the stabilizers of the Spark warship and crippled it.

Tharg spoke to them then. "I know you have no more pou sto bombs, but I invite you to fire one more time at me with anything you like. I'll even leave my vessel unprotected without shielding. Go ahead. You deserve one free shot."

Silence.

"Con Hall made a mistake. He bought a bottle of liquid he thought was old whisky. He did not know it was what it was until it was gone and he was arrested. Now he has paid for his mistake, with his life, but not before I, Scry Tharg had the honour, the privilege, the blessing of having known him. I thank you for that gift. I shall report the use of an illegal pou sto rocket by you throughout all of the galaxies. That means all of the ships in your fleets will need to be on full alert at all times henceforth since nobody travelling in your vicinity can be sure you do not have another. I expect a great many will fire on your vessels, and ask questions later. This is what you have wrought by using that bomb. You have had your pound of fiesh. Fire on me or leave. If I encounter you again, I won't thank you again. Tharg out."

"They're pulling away Captain. They might make it back home if they're careful, and do not encounter further trouble. "Tharg went below and drank a full bottle of Scaughan Dirty Dark. He had Byter cue up Bob Dylan's Dream. He cried. Deep depression set in on Tharg after that. His desire for adventure, his curiosity for the unknown waned. His existence turned sour. His life pointless. He was bitterly lonely. Lonelier than he had ever been. Ever. And that stupid line from the Bootes Helix haunted him twenty hours a shift. "Keep your hull clean Thorne."

"Excuse me Commander Thorne."

Is that you again God? What do you want from me? Why are you haunting my dreams? Why are . . .

"Captain! Captain! Wake up! It's me, Byter the Machine! Wake up Master!"

"Oh, ah, sorry Byte. I was having a bad dream again."

"First Mate Hall left you a message sir.

"What?"

"A message. In his state room on an old video camera he had salvaged out of the Junkyard, while he was cataloguing. He put a message on it for you. I don't know what it is. I knew it was there because it's plugged into the electrical system and I read the index, but it just lists . . . Goodbye Message for Captain T from First Mate Hall."

Tharg brewed coffee, strong, black coffee and sat in front of the old video playback center Con had installed in his quarters. He'd found all kinds of old movies, newsreels, press releases, of all kinds, a lot of it about Tharg and his exploits. Still in the video camera was another. Tharg took it out and put on the playback center. "Captain Tharg. I'm making this recording because when you're in such poor physical shape as I am you never know when the old ticker is going to take a long rest. I wanted to make this thing while I could. It's no big deal. I just wanted you to know that I am grateful for all you've done for me. I really enjoyed destroying all that old booze for you (He laughed). I've travelled through space with a lot of creatures, good and bad, a lot of men, good and bad, women too, but, you are the best. I don't even know why for sure. It might be because you don't really want anything. You just observe. You play. You inquire. You help. You play by the rules of honour and decency. People would be amazed at your gentleness in light of your reputation for violence. They think that's all you are. They think it all comes easy for you. They haven't seen you study. Haven't seen you practise up there on the hull. All that disgusting physical exercise (He grinned again). All those special kata with your hands, feet, weapons. They don't know you Captain. Hell, I don't really know you but I know a little. And what I know I love and I thank you for treating me to some of it and for respecting me. I don't eavesdrop Captain but I couldn't help overhearing you a few times when you were sleeping. You kept talking about your hull." You'd say, "Keep your hull clean Thorne. You'd say that a lot Captain and I don't really know what it means. Once you also said . . . You never know when it could mean the difference between Death and Life. Well Captain, I don't know about you but that saying used to read . . . You never know when it could mean the difference between Life and Death. The way you say it in your sleep Captain, it gives Death prominence. As if Death was the whole point of the saying and not Life. Somehow I think Death and the hull are connected Captain, but I don't know how. I've cleaned this hull from stem to stern, a hundred times and I don't see nothing up there to connect the two. The only thing I ever found up there besides space grime and soot was a tiny Ynnarcarbon plant growing wild under those blast vents on Seven. I think that perhaps none of it means anything Captain. It's just a bad dream. Byter can take care of that for ya if ya want. Anyway I'd just like to say thanks a lot Captain and by the way, if you're ever seeing this video then that means I'm dead and so I have a goodbye and thank-you present for you. It's in that little box on my desk over there in the corner. Hope you like it. Try to remember me for a while? And say goodbye to Shakespeare's bane for me will ya(laughs)." Tharg went over to the desk and picked up the box. Con's old cigarette lighter was there. That was one habit he'd had to give up on Lapstrake because there was no tobacco of any kind on board. He'd engraved the lighter with a few words.

To Scry Tharg
My Captain
C. Hall

The lonely swordsman took the lighter and the video with him to his own quarters. He lay down and slept and had the nightmare again. Only this time he kept thinking about his hull and that little plant growing up there. What did it mean? ~What did it have to do with anything . . .

He slept with his fist wrapped tight around the old lighter.

CHAPTER FIFTEEN

H E REMEMBERED.
Time like an ever-rolling stream bears all its sons away.

Isaac Watts. Time bore him away in 1748, not long after he wrote that. It was now the year 5,977 A.D. "Why, "Tharg wondered" hadn't time taken him away? "He was bored with his life, tired of it, desperate to die, to rest in peace. He fantasized about finding his headstone in graveyards all over the worlds. He'd invented all kinds and got a sort of peace from that. Here Lies Scry Tharg Swordsman. He lived a long and happy life. Brother! Was it long!

Nah. Not serious enough.

Herein Resteth The Remains Of
Master S. R. Tharg
Gentleman Duellist
Too pompous.
RI. P.
Scry Robert Tharg

Traveller
Better.

R. I. P.
S. R. Thorne
Father/Husband/Friend

Yes. I could live with that! But he'd have to wait. He still hadn't found a way to end his life and he had tried everything. Most of the attempts had been painful. About the only thing he hadn't tried was a pou sto bomb. He'd even tried flying into a Black Hole on a Lancer like Con Hall had done a couple of hundred years ago. But somehow, the Hole had rejected him and he had floated around in space for a long time before being picked up and returned to his abandoned ship. He didn't have the heart to destroy her. In the meantime now he had gotten involved in the Time war and was too busy to try again. The Time War was one of the most idiotic campaigns he had ever been involved in and it was having tragic consequences for the people on a small planet in a Galaxy a couple of billion miles west of Earth. Planet Osme. Small, tropical, verdant, prosperous. It had a long happy history. Its three hundred million citizens spread out and living on three of its nine continents. The other six land masses unpopulated except for a few explorers and adventurers. They weren't as hospitable as the others and were quite dangerous, some of their indigenous species of wild life violent and omnivorous. In fact, one animal on the Utnean Peninsula, the Ockovore was once brought to a major city in its infancy as a new species for the petting zoo and after it had grown, it killed and devoured one hundred and twenty-seven Osmeans before they figured out how to kill it. They destroyed it with an Osmium rifle, which was now the main source of conflict between the peoples of the three planets. Osmium was an important metal on Osme. Coming from the platinum group it was incredibly dense, so dense it had led to a common belief that Osme was once part of a

Black Hole. The Osmeans had discovered a wide array of uses for the metal, especially in weapons. The standard weapon on Osme was the Osmium rifle. It turned its targets into chunks of charred briquets.

What had brought about war was the Emperor who sits on the Ostrich throne on the largest continent, the Plates Vick Northern East. He was in love. With himself. He made Narcissus look like a veda bird, which killed itself as soon as it gave birth so that its young could have its nest and the food supply gathered before birth. Emperor Ostuum did not only fall in love with himself when he looked into a mirror. He decreed that all mirrors bear his image, so that no matter who looked into any mirror in the Empire, saw the likeness of the Emperor surrounding his own. "I want all my subjects to see, every time they gaze at my image, the heights to which they must aspire. "Now there was a religion on Osme that said there could be no work on certain sacred holy days. Unfortunately there were three of these in every nine day week. All mirrors on Osme were made from ground and polished osmium and they were in short supply. Emperor Ostuum wanted millions more made so that one and all could enjoy his countenance as often as they wished, on every possible occasion. The three-day shutdown of all industry however, made it a virtual certainty that not enough mirrors for all his subjects could be made in his lifetime. Not good enough for His Brightship. In his genius he figured out that if time were stopped at the instant the clock turned into one of these holy Sabbaths, then what followed would not be the holy Sabbath, and therefore if industries kept on working then no holy law would be broken. He decreed that this was so. That time should stop in his Empire just before the next Holy Day. The decreed also made allowances for the Sabbath Days that were being legislated out of existence, to be stored away and brought out again at that future date prescribed by the attainment of an adequate number of mirrors for each and every subject of the realm. And thus it was so decreed. This caused quite an uproar among the citizenry of Plates Vick Northern East., and its many cities. However, with the friendly persuasion of the Blackboots, the Emperor's private army, well, most people thought, after awhile, it was a great idea. Emperor Ostuum., however, was a bit embarrassed by the commotion it caused in international trade with the other continents and therefore decreed that all time should stop, everywhere by order of He, the Supreme Ostuumate, on the Ostrich Throne. War came. Tharg was hired by the King of Plates Vick West to capture Emperor Ostuum and take him into exile. The King of Slide Quator West, the other populated continent assented to this arrangement. Tharg took the assignment because of what he had heard about the Osmium rifle, that its projected tar-like fire was the same substance of the Black Holes. The war-weary swordman thought it might kill him. Send him to R. I. P land.

Getting to the Emperor had proved, so far, impossible. The Ostrich Throne was located in an underground fortress of formidable capabilities. It was protected by a vast well-trained, fully equipped, highly disciplined army, not to mention Osmium cannon batteries, that dotted the perimeter of the installation, so that there wasn't a serious space not well protected. Tharg had already absorbed several Osmium blasts. They had stopped him, brought him to his knees. For seconds only. Then he was free and his blades blurring through Osmean air. He was bitterly disappointed, but stayed to fulfill his contract. A man's word is his bond. He slept with soldiers of the other continents on board the Royal Yacht as it orbited egoland. He liked the comraderie. They questioned and teased him. He showed them sword tricks and told them old jokes he'd heard. They told him new jokes, gave him an Osmium rifle and joined in the fun of laughing at the Emperor who wanted to stop time-Some though, didn't join in. They mourned loved ones lost in the insanity of this war caused by vanity. Tharg tried to cheer them up. He told them Hans Christian Anderson's story of the Emperor's New Clothes. This cheered their hearts a little. He sang the song for them from the movie with Danny Kaye. "Isn't it oh! Isn't it ah! Isn't it absolutely grand! The King is in his altogether, his altogether, his altogether. He's altogether as naked as the day that he was born!" He broke through, after awhile to most of them and they felt better. Later some of the saddest soldiers who hadn't laughed at first, were overheard singing the lines to themselves. The King of Slide Quator West called for Tharg. He thanked him for trying to cheer the armies. "It helps a great deal Mr. Tharg." Scry blushed and turned away. Silent. The King had a new plan. It involved Tharg. He would be the centre piece. It was dangerous. It would cost many lives. The King then told Tharg something that made his heart stop. He told him that the main feature of the plan was to kill the Emperor Ostuum with the most deadly poison in the known worlds, the berries from the Ynarrcarbon plant, an almost unknown species, found only on a couple of planets. One place where it was found though, was the Utnean Peninsula. The King told Tharg he had sent for a supply and it would be here in a while. They would have to be patient.

Tharg's head was reeling. "Spook! It was on my ship all the time! On the hull! God told me. Con Hall told me. Now the King has told me. It was there all the time, I can die! I can die now!

"Are you okay Mr. Tharg. You look a little overwrought, shall I say?"

"Yes, Your Worship. Uh, I'm fine. I think I know where I can get you some of that poison a little quicker. You won't believe where it is Sir. You won't believe it.

CHAPTER SIXTEEN

Once, about three thousand years ago, Tharg worked in a Kingdom where each person was his own God. In their youth they did not know this. It had to be discovered, unaided. Only time could help. The citizens of that realm had no power until they found the truth of themselves. Then, they were a God.

That's how Tharg had felt when he had blown the thin feather dart through a vent in Emperor Ostuum's Bed chamber. The projectile was so light and thin that Emperor O did not even know he was hit. He hadn't hesitated for a second as he touched up his face in the mirror of ground Osmium before him. There were hundreds of vials and jars and tubes of ointments, unguents, oils, creams and pastes, perfumes and many other obscure beauty aids and perhaps a few with salutiferous qualities, on his rather large bureau. His entire bedchamber was a mirror. But the mirror on his bureau was a magnifier and just by leaning forward a tad, he could enlarge an eye, corner a hair, or zero in on any other part of his physiognomy. He was just so caught up in his joy, his love of his own person that he didn't notice the slight pinch in his neck as the dart did its work, entering, squirting, exiting and disintegrating, as it was designed to do. No one would ever find any physical evidence of the toxic drug that was about to take the life of the Emperor of the Ostrich Throne. Tharg had concocted the strength of the poison after he had analyzed blood and tissue samples taken from a captured relative of the Emperor, an Osmean of similar build to the ruler. He'd found the Ynarrcarbon plant right where old Con had told him on his farewell video. Tharg had gathered all of it from off his hull, finally realizing what God had been trying to tell him on that old abandoned satellite in the Bootes Helix. Death and life. Death on the hull all this time. God had known, even then what Tharg wanted. "Pilate's Fist!" He hadn't even known himself then!

Seven weeks after Tharg had given Emperor Ostuum the Ynarrcarbon cocktail, time really did stop, for him. No more Sabbatlis to worry about. No more of those nasty age wrinkles. No more stiff joints. No more insolence from his subjects or those two other minor Kings. No more trouble. Just, his beauty, everlasting. He hadn't suffered. Had never known the poison was in him at all. In fact the day his heart stopped he had written his best poem, he thought, about himself. He called it his

> Ode to Me:
> My Benediction,
> My Treasure,
> My Trial,
> My Love;
> Beauty.
> Mine.

And then his single-valve heart had exploded. Sudden sadness. Darkness.

The two Kings had offered Tharg his own continent. He'd refused. They'd offered him Ostuum's entire Empire. No dice. Finally he accepted an Osmium javelin. It was virtually indestructible, lighter than Rigan air and had been machined to limits of tolerance Tharg hadn't believed possible. It had been hand-built by three armourers who had measured Tharg and then asked him what weapon he liked next to the sword. "The jerid."

Tharg boarded Lapstrake and hit skipjack. "Head for Earth Byter.

"Are you feeling poorly Captain Thorne?"

"Head for Earth Byter. PLease.

He went below for tomato cake and tea. Then he slept and tried to make a decision. The decision.

He dreamed no more of God. No more voices. He now knew what was on his hull.

Instead, he dreamed of a small forest. A long, winding road that lead to a collection of buildings at the end of that road through that wood. An old oaken door in the main building. A nurse of some kind. Opens the door. Smiles. Says something. He can't hear, but he's always been able to read lips. Hers were the most beautiful he'd ever seen. Full, red, smiling.

"Don't do it Scry my love. My love, don't do it." Odd dream.

It took nearly six months to reach atmosphere. Earth the quiet planet they called it now. Not what it was. Not what it was. No industries now. Earth had no whaling. No seal hunt. The foxes were quiet. The dogs were quiet. No stock market. No Ford factories. No Samsung. Retirement planet Earth. A few million population. Mostly Senior Citizens living in retirement homes, all over the planet, and their staff. A few adventure tours made up a modest tourism business here and there. You could still climb Everest, but now it took only a day with the aid of an air-booster pack you wore on your back. It was against the law to climb otherwise. Enough blood had been spilled on this rock in the sea of infinite space. Earth was now Paradise. Space mariners often joked about it. "Seven days in Heaven is pure Hell. "Oh you could still rent a dory and go out and jig a codfish. There were still some left, but the population of all species, even humans, was strictly controlled at Earth's Administration Headquarters on Earth's Moon. The main body of Earthlings now lived on a planet, twenty times bigger out in the Far Eastern edges of space. But they paid to keep the old planet in good shape, careful to insure nothing of any real worth, existed there any more. Nothing that would attract the prospectors back, or the businessmen, the entrepreneurs, nothing that would start the lust for riches again, and then, the bloodshed for greed, and it would start all over again. No. Earth was a quiet retirement home. The Environment carefully restored, enhanced here and there by science, where it was unable to renew itself. It was perfectly safe now, green, warm, pretty, dull.

Tharg had a few friends there. One was a now very remote relative of Con Hall he'd encountered by accident a while ago. Another friend, Rod Dwyer, living in a retirement home on Bell Island, in Conception Bay, Newfoundland was, as far as Tharg could determine, the last Newfoundlander left on Earth. Since Tharg was also a Newfoundlander by birth, he liked to visit Mr. Dwyer and hear all the news and tell a few tales of his own. Dwyer loved it and Tharg always brought him a different bottle of booze each time, from some far off place or another. This time it was black whisky brewed on Osme and contained in a polished flask of Osmium glass. He'd tasted it and had shortly afterwards stabbed himself in the foot with his own sword. Dwyer would love it.

He put Lapstrake into orbit around the Moon and asked for permission to visit Earth. Personal. "We have had quite a number of new complaints about you Mr. Tharg. There are even rumours that a formal Bill of Indictment has been issued against you claiming you have stolen an entire Federal Prison and assassinated its Chief Warden. As well, the Sparks have charged you with treason, interference, and slander. Lately there have been rumours as well that you started a war in the Osmean sector and those are just a few of the complaints coming in against you sir. You have been busy."

"I request permission to visit Earth on a personal matter. The standard fee has already been desposited in your treasury and I have a special gift, sent to your Commander from Emperor Vess on Riga-"

"Oh yes, that was another rumour I was told to ask you about Mr. Tharg, about the Kaltic Spallows, or the Spalling or whatever they are called. Is it true you have one on board, because if you do they would be quite illegal in this air space?"

"No. I don't have one. Do those things really exist? I thought that was a fairy tale."

"Permission granted to visit Earth Mr. Tharg. If you have any mail or correspondence of any kind for this station or our Commander please send it on a Facteur Shuttle at once. Out and behave yourself Swordsman."

"Thank you Major and please give my best to Commander Nugent. The shuttle is on its way."

One other thing Commander Tharg. About Blax. Thank you."

"Belinda is ready. She's aboard the Lancer. Will you be long sir?"

"Thanks Byter. I don't know how long I'll be. I'm going to my cabin for awhile for a nap. I'll leave when dusk comes to Earth. Pipe in that Radio Station that plays all those old hits will ya?"

"C-WAS. Very well Commander. Sleep tight. Don't let the bugs bite."

"You said it twenty-seven hundred days, four hours and twelve seconds ago, after that party on "Shhhh. I remember Byte. Good night." "Sir."

Decisions. Decisions. Tharg sat in his cabin listening to the Animals singing Oh Lord Please Don't Let Me Be Misunderstood. What a voice that guy had. Before that he'd heard The Idiot by Stan Rogers. He'd hoped that wasn't an omen. He had a hypodermic syringe in his hand. It was filled with a light grey liquid. Enough posion to kill him in fifteen months. He figured it would take him that long to get used to the idea he was going to die, to enjoy that feeling, say goodbye and pretend he was living a normal life and dying a normal death. He hadn't taken it yet. When he had returned to his cabin he'd slept for a few hours. The Golden Oldies always lulled him into a deep sleep. He'd had a few weird dreams though. In one, a God in a fire storm had been saying something to him he couldn't quite get. It might have been. "Don't. I have a gift for you now!" But he wasn't sure. In another dream he saw that nurse again. The one with the lips. In the last dream he'd been floating in space, holding hands with Con Hall. They were laughing and carrying on, drinking and singing old Newfoundland folksongs, especially We'll rant and we'll roar like true Newfoundlanders.

He'd slept to consider. Now his decision was made. He had lived for nearly four thousand years. It wasn't right. That's not why he had gone to Dr. Brougham. All he'd ever wanted was to live out his life with his wife Isabel and his child and grand-children. That's all. Not this. All that time. All those wars. Those battles. All that blood. He could still picture the Scaderk warrior trying to get back his own severed limb as it floated away on his blood. Tharg shivered. Not right. The Endurions were right. He was an abomination. He was going to beat Krit Thelm to the punch after all. Major Nugent had told him Thelm was searching the universes for him, and kept coming back to Earth at regular intervals to check. He had said he was due back again. Too late now Thelm Old Var. Tharg plunged the needle into his upper thigh. He drained the syringe. He looked at his Ironman Chronometer. Fifteen months to go. Time to say goodbye. He felt at peace. He knew he'd made the right choice. Peace was rare for him. He welcomed it in.

Belinda roared up over the hill from the ferry terminal on Bell Island. The pavement had long ago disintegrated and now the roads were dust again. Before long Tharg was covered with the red dust that came from the ore Bell Island had once been famous for. A low grade iron ore mined in tunnels three miles under the island and out into Conception Bay. With the advent of surface mining and higher grade ores in Labrador and elsewhere the mines had closed. People had left the Island and the small town of Wabana. Now it was just another retirement haven, although it did have one of the best restaurants on Earth in the old mine shaft at Scotia Ridge. The Miner's Lunch. Yummy! Bell Island stew . L'Anse Cove dumplings. Neary cake. Excellent! He'd go there later after he saw Rod Dwyer, and had a little swallow with him. He went to the old lighthouse first though. Actually the ruins of the old light at the back of the island. Years ago you could always see humpback whales from the light if you had the patience to wait a while. Tharg always checked, but he hadn't seen one in his last three visits. He got off Belinda and walked over to the old fence that protected, visitors from the sheer drop to the ocean below. He stared out at the blue grey ocean. It was calm. He was overwhelmed again by deja vu. Today it took him right back to the time he used to come here with his sisters and his grandfather Parsons. They'd always see whales. Suddenly the calm of the ocean was gone as two huge humpbacks broke the flatness. In slow motion. Kodak grace. It seemed they took forever to complete the cycle of their dive up through the surface and then down. Like a giant wheel, ever so slowly. Tears filled Tharg's eyes. "What hath God wrought. "He was surprised that he still remembered the Old Book. It had been important to him once, an age ago. The whales kept coming up for air and heading out to sea and after a while, they were gone. Good luck! It's a good luck day today!

The Miner's Memorial Retirement Home was located in a small forest, at the end of a pretty road on the Bell Meadow where a few wild horses, still roamed. They were fed by the state now, of course. Tharg roared up to the parking lot in a cloud of dust that followed him all the way up to the door. As he stepped out of it to ring the doorbell, the door opened and a woman stepped out. The most beautiful women he had ever seen, anywhere. The nurse, from his dreams. She stood there with shock written all over her face. Her mouth wide open in astonishment. All she could say was, 'You! It's you!'

Then she smiled.

CHAPTER SEVENTEEN

"MY NAME IS Scry Tharg. I have come to visit my old friend Rod Dwyer. May I come in?"

Her hair was black as a a Cuban's, eyes deep set, hooded, stars in them, short upturned nose, voluptuous lips, naturally red, a smile lingered there. Full figure and she was tall, healthy looking. Tanned. Probably a runner.

She was blushing. He was blushing.

"Mr. Tharg, please. Come in."

As Tharg entered and pulled the heavy oak door behind him he asked, "What did you mean when you said "You! "when you saw me?"

They had entered a small sitting room. She sat down at a little desk covered with papers and envelopes and writing material. Tharg sat in an old fashioned wooden chair with a high back. "I dreamed of you. I, I saw you in my dreams." "That's odd. I dreamed of you too, but only recently. It seemed you were trying to tell me something. I couldn't get what it was. Are you the new Manager here? Is Mrs. Trickett retired now?" "No. I'm a nurse. Mrs. Trickett is in town picking up fuel tubes for the furnace."

She was sitting straight up, hands in her lap, neat, formal, proper. She studied the tall man sitting before her and looking oddly out of place, sitting. He had curious scars and his eyes were so blue. Deep as Conception Bay. He was built like a soccer player, but taller, more muscular above, but not the kind of bulk weight lifters carried. He moved like a squirrel. Fast, quick motions and stops as if he'd learned not to Waste energy, almost everything he did was as fluid as quicksilver. He was the most attractive man she'd ever seen.

"I love your Harley Davidson Fat Boy. Don't see many now. There are none on Bell Island."

Tharg was trying not to stare at her. It was hard. Looking at her was easier than eating tomato soup cake with lassie sauce. It was such a treat. He was surprised she recognized Belinda. Not many people knew what they were anymore. 'I call her Belinda.' A long time ago, an uncle had a bike that was his favourite and he called his bike Belinda. So I sort of stole the name. She's a 1340 Fat Boy, 1990 Model." "Yes I know. 1388 cc, four-strike 45 degree V-twin engine. Puts out about 59 horsepower at 4800 rpms-Primary chain transmission, 628 pounds, maximum speed 106 mph. Very nice.

Tharg was amazed. "Actually she can do 130 now because of a few modifications I've made but how do you know all that Mrs . . . ah?

"I'm sorry. My name is Maudie Parsons, Nurse Maudie Parsons. I have a photographic memory, unenhanced. I'm sort of hung up about the old days and old things. The home here has a vast library of books and as well, the computers are hooked up to Omninet which carries almost everything about everything that ever was and I read a lot. I like old things. I regret the passing away from our world of so many things that were so good, so long ago Mr. Tharg. How do you feel about the old days. Do you know much about them? Have you read much about them?" Tharg stared at her. "Yes, I know a bit about the old days." They sat there talking, but mostly absorbing. Inhaling each other's presence. The world had ceased to exist beyond the three feet of Earth air that encircled them.

And up above Bell Island. Above the clouds. Up above the orbiting Lapstrake. Above the Earth's solar system and above all the other systems higher than that. High, high up above and beyond the tip of the worlds, a God with eyes like fire storms looked down, way down to Earth at the man and the woman. "Now you have your gift Tharg the Emancipator. I have laid it in your hand. Now enjoy it while you can son. This is your reward for my freedom."

"Well I guess I better have a visit with Dwyer now, but I'd sure like to talk with you again M'am.

She tried not to stare and instead, to concentrate on his words so that would preoccupy her and preclude staring, but it was hard. She was in love with this man she had met one hour ago! Impossible and ludicrous!

"Oh. Sorry Mr. Tharg. I forgot. I have bad news for you. Mr. Dwyer passed away three weeks ago. He left you a little note. I have it here."

She pulled open the top drawer of the little desk and withdrew the letter.

"I'm sorry. I tried to get back as soon as I could because I knew he was getting weaker. I'll just look at the note later thank you. I'll go now I guess."

Tharg tucked the letter into his belt as if it were a knife.

"Um, where is Mr. Dwyer now, um his you know?" "Oh! He lies buried in the meadow Mr. Tharg. I could take you there if you wish."

"Yes. Okay. Thank you."

They left the home and walked out to the meadow, inside the small wood. The meadow was actually a low rise, a hill that ended on a sheer cliff overlooking the bay. Mr. Dwyer's grave was covered with fresh flowers, lily of the valley and hyacinths. The nurse stayed behind a respectable distance as Tharg visited the resting place of the second-last Newfoundlander. He knelt down on the soft grass and touched the rough, white headstone. Put his fingers in the recessed carving of the name.

"You have a good long rest Old Son."

He stayed there fifteen minutes. His eyes were still wet when he left the graveside. Maudie looked away. "Lord what a sweet, tender man! He seems so sad and lonely. He holds his loneliness like arms held in front of his face protecting his soul."

Tharg walked over to her then. He looked into her eyes for a long time. This time she looked into his. For a long time. They just studied each other and learned and felt and knew. Then Tharg put his hand down and took hers. It was cool. His was rough. They turned and walked away, along the edge of the cliff. He picked a buttercup and rolled it under her chin. "You really like butter don't you?" She took the buttercup and put her hand behind his head and kissed him. It was a long, deep drink. "I think I've been looking for you for four thousand years Maudie. I have a long story to tell you. The ending contains bad news, and good news." "Could you tell me the bad news first?" He looked into her eyes and deep into her soul. He saw strength in there, a strength she would need now. "Well, okay. Do you know what a Ynarrcarbon plant is Maudie and is there a priest on Bell Island?"

They walked away, hand in hand. He told her a long story. A tale that would end in fifteen months.

"Scott, let's do it this, way. I have learned long ago that regret is a corrosive time waster. There are some things we cannot change. But we can change the way we accept them. Let us not regret, you and I, that we have only fifteen months together. Let us hold our love in our hearts and hands like the delicate, beautiful thing it is and cherish it, and spend it, and let it go out of us into the world, and let it make us and the world and all the worlds so full of joy that our love will become greater than all of the worlds and escape time and laugh at time and scorn time for what it is, nothing. Time is nothing. We are something Tharg, you and I. Us, is something. I I love you man from the sky! Oh, I love you! I breathe you Tharg, old man. I give you me. I give you us. Here take my blood, my life, my heart. Be Scottie! Be! You and I!"

And so they took the gift the God had given them at face value. They took it and swallowed it and used it up, even though it could never run out. They splashed in it. Wallowed in it. Paraded in it. Ate it. Slept it. Cried it sometimes, because sometimes they cried. For joy, for their gift and not for the future, or the past, but just for them and their being. Their is.

They got married in the little Chapel at the home where Maudie was nurse and warlord. A young Pastor from St. John's came over on the ferry. Tharg picked him up on Belinda and they thundered their way to the chapel. Scott had made himself a tuxedo Circa 1990. Cummberbund, bow-tie, silk lapels, the works. He also made Maudie a deep burgundy velvet dress with matching cape and hood. He was a superb tailor and seamstress and this made Maudie giggle and clap her hands with amazement. "Oh buddy. I'm going to tell people I knows you!" she'd say. Tharg would say, "Don't you mean I know you, the singular verb agreeing with the single pronoun I." "Ah Scottie! That's not the way old Mr. Dwyer used to talk boy! He used to say that to me whenever I'd do something he thought would make me famous, like reciting the entire New Testament for him or the Red Books of Agg. He'd say . . . "I knows you!"

"Do you Maudie Parsons take this man to be your lawfully wedded husband . . . "With all of my being, I do."

"Do you Scott Robert Thorne take this woman to be your lawfully wedded wife?"

"Try and stop me mister."

"Scottie!"

"Oops. Sorry. Sometimes certain words and tones make me regress. Ask me again please."

"Do you Scott Robert Thorne take this woman to be your lawfully wedded wife?"

"As God is my witness, as Emperor Vess is my witness, the Kaltic Spallows, Con Hall, as Byter is my witness, with all of my heart, I do, I do, oh sir, I do!"

"Then by the power invested in me by the Federal Licensing Agencies I now pronounce you Man and wife. Mr. and Mrs. Scott Robert Thorne. The Thornes."

"The Thargs." Maudie shouted and said, "And now you may kiss the groom!", and that's exactly what she did.

Tharg paid the Pastor with a gem from Albion's State Treasury that would probably allow him to build fifty churches.

They honeymooned everywhere. Lisbon, Paris, London, Heidleberg, Nain, Moscow, Mokpo, Zermatt, Perth, and elsewhere. He found another Harley Davidson for her, a 1993 Sportster and they roared through the cities of the earth. They slept on beaches, mountain tops, desert islands, in the middle of the Sahara and in an Eco-Tent on the Moon.

They kissed often, everywhere, reverently and with great joy, everywhere. As if they were trying to describe their own bodies to each other and how it worked. Awe and joy. And reverence. Perfect love. Maudie made up corny sayings. Love means you never allude."

Tharg countered with "Love means you never eat beans on your honeymoon."

"That's gross! Love means you know what's coming."

"Love means Maudie Parsons, Nurse, a. k. a Maudie Tharg, wife."

"Oh Scottie. Scry honey. One year after they got married, while they were having a campfire on Lapstrake's Port wing, Byter reported that a message was incoming from Moon Base. Major Nugent. "Commander Tharg. The Endurion, Krit Thelm, has found you."

CHAPTER EIGHTEEN

"IT'S NOTHING TO worry about Maudie. He can't get to me before my time is up and after that it won't matter."

Maudie seemed pre-occupied.

"A shekel for your cogitations? "he asked.

The puzzled look on her face. "It's an old way of asking someone what's on their mind."

Oh! I have heard one like that. A penny for your thoughts. Scott. I've got something to tell you. It's going to be a little hard to explain. I don't even know if it's important but, you said the other day love means there are no surprises, so.

"Well. You're not an ungulate are you?"

"No I'm not whatever that is, but, I am a meme.

"Meme? On dit meme. C'est la meme chose? Meme. Alorsl"

"Scry. Give that up. I'm being serious. A meme is a person who can change into another person. Can become that person. Can be that person. The time you can be another person varies. For me it's seven seconds. There. Maudie meme is the French word for our word-same. C'est la meme chose. It is the same thing. Meme. But honey I'm not sure what you mean. What do you mean?"

Then Tharg saw one of the most amazing sights he had ever seen, and he had seen a lot of amazing sights. Maudie stood up and before he could discern any change, any movement, anything, Rod Dwyer was standing before him speaking.

"Scott honey, this is what I meant. I will be Rod for another three seconds." Then, Maudie was standing before him. Looking pensive, worried, upset. Upsot, as Rod used to say. Suddenly Tharg started dancing up and down, howling, hooting, clapping his hands, laughing. Worse than Tom Cruise. He did a little dance and sang, "Oh crawdaddy fish, oh crawdaddy fish! Yippee. Hallelujah! If that don't beat all. "Then he rushed over and started kissing and hugging Maudie and throwing her up in the air. Oh! Honey I love you. All of you. The more the merrier. That was great honey. Who else can you do?"

Tharg was staring at a mirror. Except it was moving and saying, "Oh crawdaddy fish, oh crawdaddy fish.

Tharg went into another frenzy of delight. Grabbed a sword, blurred through the air with it so fast all Maudie saw was a moving rainbow of colour. She did Elvis. "And another litle baby boy was born in the ghetto." Tharg shrieked with joy.

Maudie told him the story, after he calmed down. A few years ago, she'd had a special patient. A man named Armon Bar. He said he was from Northern India. He was retired and wanted to live on Bell Island because he preferred to spend his last years in a cool climate. He'd said his late wife Ferial had come from a northern place. He became a little enamoured of Maudie, probably because she took such good care of all her charges at the home. Maudie had noticed that Mr. Bar was a very spiritual man and read many books. He prayed and was devout and pious. To her, he seemed a very holy person. Sometimes he'd read beautiful words to her while she was sitting with him. She repeated her favourite that she remembered. Then she recited it, she became Armon Bar so that Tharg could see his kindly face and remember him too. She did him. "Awake! For Morning in the Bowl of Night Has flung the Stone that puts the Stars To Flight:

And Lo! The Hunter of the East has caught The Sultan's Turret in a Noose of Light."

She had finished the last few lines as Maudie. "I know that, "Tharg said, "It's from the Rubaiyat of Omar Khayyam. Very beautiful. He had a kind face that man." Maudie went on with her story. She told Tharg that when he was on his death bed, she had spent many, many hours with him, bathing him and giving him cool sips of juices and ices. In his last hour on Earth he had asked her for a great favor, and at the same time asked permission to give her, in return, a gift. She thought he was going to give her a book of poems, or something else from his book collection so she agreed. The favour that he had asked her was to lie down beside him on the bed, as his wife used to do, so that he could put his arms around her and pretend to say goodbye to his beloved Ferial. Just for a second or two he said. Maudie, with her heart of gold and out of control romantic nature didn't bat an eye lash. Hopped up on the bed. He put his arms around her. He closed his eyes. Asked her to close her eyes. As she did he said, "Goodbye my darling Ferial. Wife of my soul."

Maudie got up out of the bed and told him brightly, "That was sweet. I hope it made you glad and gay Mr. Bar. "He looked at her and thanked her and told her he hoped she would enjoy the gift he had given her. "Um, which gift is that Mr. Bar?"

"Go look in the mirror Nurse Parsons. And tell Me what you see."

She humoured him. "I see me Mr. Bar. Just me."

"Keep looking in the mirror Nurse Parsons and, just to humour me, while you are staring at yourself, pretend you see me, instead.

Maudie had shrugged her shoulders and said okay. She saw Mr. Bar staring back in the mirror.

"How did you do that Mr. Bar? That was amazing!"

"I didn't do it Maudie. You did."

"Oh come on now Mr. Bar. I think you're having a spell codding me now ain't ya? "She talked like Mr. Dwyer sometimes when carrying on.

"Why don't you look at yourself in the mirror Maudie and pretend you see someone I could not possibly ever have known."

"Mr. Bar this is getting kind of spooky now, would you like a bath?"

"Please Maudie just this last thing."

Maudie shrugged her shoulders, turned to the mirror and pretended to see her sister Rosslyn, who had left Earth for the new Earth three years ago. Rosslyn stared back at her!

"You see Scry. Mr. Bar was a meme. He was many things actually, I can't imagine what else he was, but he was a meme. He could become someone for a little while and when I lay there in that bed with him pretending to be his wife, he changed me into her for seven seconds so that he could say goodbye to her and then I became a meme, because once you did it once, that's it. You are. I just thought you might like to know that about me."

As she was finishing her story Mrs. Trickett, Maudie's boss at the home contacted the ship. She had some bad news for them. The young Pastor who had married them was missing and some creep calling himself Phil Elm or something, claimed to have him. He said if Mr. Tharg didn't come at once to the Bell Island ferry terminal the young cleric would become another Scry Tharg victim.

"It never rains but it pours. "Tharg said and was about to leave when he had a great idea. "Maudie. Do me again."

It was raining and blowing and Thelm was getting sick. The Earth weather was worse than abominable. However, it would be over soon and he would have his revenge on the abominate. A revenge uglier than anything the human could imagine. The young Pastor stood by his side in a slight metabol trance. Thelm had no desire to cause the young Earthling's death, but would if he was forced by circumstance. He looked up and suddenly, he could see the cursed swordsman standing over near some shipping crates. Visibility was poor in this driving rain. "Walk over to me Tharg and this child can live out his years." "Let him come to me, half-way Thelm. That's how we do these things here. On good faith. I'll come half-way. He'll come half-way. Then I'll come all the way. You can keep your metal-projector aimed at him all the while until you touch me. Fair enough?

Thelm studied the area carefully. There was nothing between the two except a few crates and boxes. He'd handle this with extreme prejudice.

"Very well thief. Begin!"

Tharg started forward. Thelm pushed the dazed Pastor forward and he started walking toward Tharg. The rain was blowing hard. Visibility was poor. Then, Tharg was standing in front of him and the Pastor was gone. No matter. He had Tharg. He dropped his metab-projector and brought up another weapon and aimed it at his chest. "What!" It wasn't aimed at Tharg's chest at all but a young female Earthling in some kind of uniform. Who are you and where is Tharg? "He screamed. I am Nurse Maudie Parsons and I am on my way to a mission of mercy. I have never heard of a Tharg. I was walking through this driving rain from the ferry and the next thing I know you have that monstrosity stuck in my face. Would you mind telling me why you are threatening me sir?"

"Threatening you? I'm not, I don't even know you Earthling. I want to know, did you see a man here just a moment ago?"

"Why yes I believe I saw the young Pastor from a local church but I can't see him now." She looked around searching with her eyes. Then she looked back at Thelm. "You're not from the Moon Base are you sir?" Thelm lowered the weapon. He turned from her and went away. As he did he heard that ugly sound again. The ugliest sound in the Universes. Laughter. Only it wasn't the Xe tzrect this time. This time it was a female's laughter! In lavic rage, Thelm realized he'd been duped, tricked by the abominate and, and now he realized, his new bride. The very woman that young religionist he'd abducted had married to Tharg. In his rage, he couldn't see where he was going. That's when he went overboard, into the icy waters of Conception Bay, where Rod Dwyer used to swim, as a boy. Of the two, Rod was the more graceful swimmer.

"Here's to you as good as you are, and here's to me as bad as I am, and as bad as I am and as good as you are, I'm as good as you are as bad as I am." Maudie laughed heartily as she taught Tharg the new toast. Tharg laughed and roared and could hardly sit still. The young Pastor had been returned to his home safely. Moon Base had ordered Thelm off the planet and were now carefully monitoring his whereabouts and Maudie and Paula were continuing their honeymoon. "You know Mrs. Thorne, that little talent of yours could prove a definite asset keeping this marriage together. Yes indeed. Catspit! That was funny" Oh Scotty you should have heard the bile in his queer little voice as he asked me if I'd seen you around anywhere. And I'm sure I heard the strangest screaming ever, followed by a large splash as I laughed my way back to you. That was good sport darling. Here's to ya!" Tharg toasted and saluted her all night. In the back of his mind though, lie tried to figure out what kind of a weapon Thelm was carrying as described by Maudie. He couldn't place it at all. Oh well. "Here's to you Nurse Parsons Tharg on behalf of all the beleaguered seniors in the world who now have to do without your services." Then they went up on the hull for a weenie roast.

CHAPTER NINETEEN

"I HAVE BEEN COM-MANDED to end the obscenity you call your life Scry Tharg. By high order and decree of the Spar Tr, White Mane and with the assent of all the peoples of Endurion I am so ordered." Krit Thelm's alien voice box gave all of the words a nasal resonance as if he was trying to say the word "no" but was stuck on the I have been commanded, making that sound continuously. Innnn havennnn beennnnnn commandednnnnn . . . He had a multi-armed darthook pistol aimed directly at Tharg who was standing six feet away at Lapstrake's Control Room Keyboard Panel. Tharg was frozen, utterly motionless, a position he found optimum for unleashing one of his offensive moves. He did not speak, but let Thelm do all the talking, make all the moves until he was ready. Tharg was confident of his own matchless speed. "You should never have interfered in my life Tharg-Karnor Val Po was mine. Mine! I won her fair and square. A Potlatch is not human Tharg so why should you have bothered anyway? Her human trait was her body, not her genetic carriage. She was of no concern to you. She was not human and she was mine! I wanted her. She was mine. I would have made her very happy. A Queen if she wanted it. Mine. My property! "He shifted position so slightly that Maudie, who was standing next to Tharg, but closer to Thelm, didn't notice. Neither did she notice Tharg as he adjusted his stance slightly to accomodate the new positon Thelm had taken. Their moves were so fast and subtle, few but the highly trained could notice. Tharg knew instantly that Thelm had positioned himself into a stance more suitable for a head blast. He is going to try to put a dart into Tharg's head. "Make your move Thelm." "Tharg hadn't budged as he spoke, ever so quietly. "Go ahead Cyc, kill me if you can."

"I'd laugh Earthling if Endurions laughed. You'd love that wouldn't you? Death. You'd embrace it like Terran air wouldn't you Tharg. Oh, don't worry. You're going to get your due shortly. I might have been more merciful this year if you hadn't taken what was mine!

Suddenly Maudie did Schwarzenegger "I'll be back," and took a vicious swing at Thelm while she had all that bulk. But in a blur Tharg had pulled her behind him and as she came out of the meme she saw that no one but she had budged. But Tharg knew better. Although she had not observed it, he had seen Thelm bring his weapon up, aim it at her head, just as he was pulling her behind him, and as he was letting go her arm, Thelm had returned to his original position, prepared to strike at Tharg's head. She was pale and shaken, but didn't move, not knowing what else to do. She had to figure some way of protecting her man though.

"You are the Xe tzrect, the abominate Tharg," Thelm went on. "The filth of an Earth science that shouldn't even exist. An unholy evil to every known Deity Tharg. You can't care much for that poor nurse behind you to risk her life by even knowing you. Oh I know you think you can protect her, but can you? Can you even protect yourself? I have a very big surprise for you Whistler. Perhaps the second biggest surprise of your dirty, ugly life. You wish to know what it isnnnnnn?"

Silence.

Maudie was so afraid and nervous that she thought she'd throw up. Tharg sensed her anxiety. "Don't move honey. "Thelm rippled with disgust. "Honey. How sweet. How romantic. How tragic. How fatal. Okay. I'll tell you what the surprise is Tharg, since you can't do anything to stop it now anyway, you nor anyone else. You think I'm here to kill you don't you? Indeed, I have been commanded to so do by my own Commander-in-Chief. However, my people do not yet understand what the real state of affairs is with you Knifelancer. I have been following you for a very long time now and I know something about you that not many other people know, perhaps nobody knows, besides Krit Thelmnnnnn. I know Tharg that you seek and pray for death the way you once sought life and its forces, but I have come to give you everlasting immortality Tharg. I have come to make you live until all others, all civilizations have passed away Tharg. When I fire this weapon at you, you will never die. Not even the Ynarrcarbon plant will harm you Tharg! Did not know I knew did you Tharg? But now you will begin your eternal life of hell by living Tharg. You'll not only bury that nurse but a million more like her Tharg and every time you do you'll remember my gift to you Tharg. My special gift-Life!"

At the instant Thelm fired, Maudie had decided and acted. She did an Orion squirrel, the fastest creature in all the worlds. Jumped from Tharg's shoulder, just as he moved, and directly into the line of fire. One dart hit her and knocked her to the floor as Tharg disabled all the others with his blade. They went everywhere except into him or Maudie.

At the same instant Thelm had turned to flee Tharg smashed his blade across his skull and behind the mandible sac. Thelm hit the floor like a drunk, unconscious. Tharg turned from Thelm as Maudie was coming to. A dart was in her shoulder. She felt fine. She pulled the dart and threw it. She hadn't seen Thelm fall and her dart hit him high in his torso. Something like a scream came from him as he came to-Tharg and Maudie looked at him with a strange kind of sympathy. "I don't want to hurt you Thelm. Karnor wasn't a human being, but no one has the right to enslave another, nowhere, no way, no how, ever. I don't know how you got on board my ship but you can take a Lancer bike and get the hell off now before I change my mind. If you had hurt my woman I'd be curing you in the hot sun as we speak. Go now!"

Maudie was rubbing her shoulder. There was a tiny hole in it where the dart had hit her. She stared at Thelm. "Karnor deserved better than you Endurion and by the way, she got it." It was the closest to a snarl Tharg had ever heard come out of his gentle, crazy nurse with the big memory. "Get thee hence!" she finally shouted.

It sounded like Thelm was wheezing but then they both realized he was saying something. Tharg finally picked it out and repeated it. "Ke tzrect. Ke tzrect. "Maxidie was puzzled and looked at Scry with a "Well? "written all over her face. "He's saying Ke tzrect, Thelm the abominate, Thelm the Abominate. I think that dart you threw at him did to him whatever he thought it was going to do to me, and, if I figure it right, I think it also means he did it to you too. I believe it all means both you and Thelm are now immortal."

Maudie grabbed Tharg by the arm. "Scry you've got to get a dart and use it on yourself. You'll be cured if it works as he claims. Do it!"

Thelm spoke again then. "What do you mean cured? He can't die you fool! He's the xe tzrect, the abominate!" Maudie looked at the Cyclid. Then she told him Tharg was dying. Thelm stared into her eyes for a long time. He rippled. After a while he understood. And was glad. "So. Tharg. You are going to die after all and I almost stopped it. Now when you want to live more than anything I almost gave you the greatest gift ever given in any circumstance since the worlds began, your life back. Some Endurion God must have foiled my game. It is almost worth it now to endure what I must endure forever, just to know that my revenge on you will come anyway. Oh, that is so good THARG! And I promise you I will not leave undone the work that needs to be done to your friend there for what she has done to me. Oh no."

As he uttered the threat to Maudie Tharg blurred into motion. His blade spun threw the artificial air at Thelm's head. But, the Endurion had vanished! He was gone. The appropriate cliche would be, thin air.

A few hours later in the lab Tharg discovered that only one of the darts had had a special ingredient. The others were untreated. Thelm had vanished with the other dart still in his upper body. No dice. No reprieve. He could have cried.

Then, Maudie did.

CHAPTER TWENTY

"I REMEMBER A LINE from a poem in one of my daughter's school books. The poem was The Wanderer. The first line went: This lonely traveller longs for Grace, for the mercy of God. That's how I feel today. I feel badly in need of Grace." He coughed again. Tharg was lying on his cot in a sleeping cubicle on Deck Two. Lapstrake was nestled between two mountain ranges in the Swiss Alps under a million tons of newly fallen snow. She did John Wayne. "Well I'm sorry I called ya a chili-dipping horse thief fella".

Scry laughed again. Coughed.

"Want water honey?"

"No. I want what I've always had longevity without end, with you".

Maudie came over and bit his ear. "Want to make a little immortal?"

He laughed. He said "I thought we'd have made a dozen by now. Perhaps Brougham screwed that up when he re-tread my genes."

"I don't think so hon." She was leaning against one of the tall helical portholes. She could hear Lapstrake. It seemed to be murmuring. Weeping.

"I should have killed Thelm a long time ago. First when I met him. When he was trying to kill that Potlatch."

"You mean Karnor?"

"Yeah. Karnor".

"Did you love her?"

"Uh, ah, no. no I didn't."

"You mean you loved her but didn't love her."

"Very good Maudie. I'm starting to like you."

She did Stallone, "Go for it."

He laughed again and this time he didn't cough. That made him feel better. "You have to be extremely careful now. Thelm is not finished with you. He hated me more than anyone was ever hated and now he hates you even more. Also the Endurions, well they'll send another when they find out he failed. What they'll do when they find out what you did to Thelm I couldn't possibly say, but it won't be pleasant."

"Perhaps I'll go find him and kill him myself."

"Maudie, please. Don't even joke about that okay? There's only one way to kill him now and only the Endurions know what it is. If I had saved some of the Ynarrcarbon we could mix you up another batch and take him that way, but, I took it all. I wanted to make sure.

"You did. You made sure Scry."

She turned away from him as she filled up.

"Another thing Maudie. You have to keep track of Thelm. He still seeks revenge and my death won't stop him, especially if he finds out about you."

"I'm not afraid of Thelm." Maudie I stuck the Charm in him about fifty times and didn't kill him. He's a monster! A dragon! The bogeyman!" "The what?"

"Just keep track of him honey and remember there are many people in debt to him who can never repay what they owe and he owns those people. They'll do whatever he tells them to, especially if he promises to forgive their debts and they're foolish enough to believe him.

Maudie was wearing her red velvet dress with hood and cape and long black boots. It was his favourite.

"You look like Little Red Riding Hood, "He told her with love eyes.

"Thank you Master Swordsman."

"Oh Maudie if I'd only kept even one Spalling Lark! Just one. One wouldn't have been so bad would it?" The anguish in his voice choked her psyche.

"If you had then you wouldn't be Tharg."

"Well I never asked to be Tharg in the first place!" He shouted. It was the first time she'd ever heard him raise his voice like that.

Silence.

"Want me to bring down Belinda?"

"Nah. There's no point if I can't ride her. She's yours now Maudie. I hope you'll keep her. Just be careful on her. She's fast that lady. "He was staring at her now and couldn't take his eyes off her.

"Could you just come here? "He whispered.

She came over and sat by him and held him. He spoke to her in French for a long time and told her of his love for her and how he would have missed her so much all those years in space if he had known of her. She didn't understand a word he said but understood everything. He told her this last Christmas with her was the most beautiful in his memories. They'd found a small stand of evergreen trees high up in a Swiss meadow on one of the mountains and he had Byter build him a component log cabin. They put it in the meadow and stayed there for the twelve days of Christmas. They even had a tree all decorated and gave each other presents. Tharg gave her a portable video machine and an ancient version of the movie A Christmas Carol starring Alastair Sim and Kathleen Harrison. They watched it a dozen times and cried every time at the end. She gave Tharg an old Earth watch, a Bulova, that still worked. It had been a gift to her from a patient years ago. Tharg loved it and put it on right away and liked to listen to it ticking They sang Christmas Carols, as many as they could remember. Tharg had a twelve string guitar and played along. He especially liked Gabriel's Message, and they sang that a lot. He'd always loved the line: Then gentle Mary meekly bowed her head, to me be as it pleaseth God she said." "Great attitude that girl." Tharg said. "I thought you were an atheist Christmas Boy?" Maudie poked at him.

He looked out the window of the log cabin at the stars. "So did I." She didn't press him on it. It had been a lovely holiday.

Tharg started to cough again and Maudie gave him another injection. He slept for a while. She was worried about Thelm. She didn't know how she was going to do on her own once Scry was gone. He was so good. In so many ways still a little boy. A little boy who never grew up. Who could never grow up. Didn't want to. He's like Peter Pan! Except he'd found out the hard way that Never Never Land wasn't pretty. She held his rough hands. They'd been so strong and fast! And gentle, tender, exciting. Tears rolled down her cheeks and splashed on his hands. Like Extreme Unction.

Tharg died then.

She buried him in Corner Brook, his first home, near where he'd always believed his first wife and daughter were buried long ago. So long ago.

She got back on board Lapstrake. She told Byter to take her to the Bootes Helix Field. And then it did.

The End

CPSIA information can be obtained at www.ICGtesting.com
Printed in the USA
LVOW08s0324030813

346120LV00001B/16/P